International Acclaim for

"If there is a posterity, *The Good Do[ctor]* [will be one of the] great literary triumphs of South Africa's transition, a book in every way the equal of J. M. Coetzee's *Disgrace*. . . . [Galgut is] a novelist of great and growing power."
—Rian Malan, author of *My Traitor's Heart*

"Of the younger generation [of South African novelists], Galgut, with his spare, unhurried sentences, his carefully chosen words, is the most talented." —*The Economist* (London)

"[*The Good Doctor* is] expressed in spare, tough prose that can sketch deftly the behavior of both inanimate things and people . . . This eye for the particular plays a large part in Damon Galgut's achievement. It is the contradictions and strange details of his bleak landscape that lend compulsiveness to *The Good Doctor's* serious concerns."
—*The Times Literary Supplement* (London)

"Apartheid is over, but its sad afterbirth remains. . . . [The] visit to the homeland's former dictator, now in hiding, [is] a haunting portrait of the melancholy of deposed evil." —*The New York Times*

"At a time when much so-called 'literary' fiction has settled into fulfilling comfortable expectations, *The Good Doctor* unsettles and confounds. There are traces of J. M. Coetzee and Graham Greene but Damon Galgut is a true original."
—Geoff Dyer, author of *Out of Sheer Rage*

"Galgut spins a brisk and bracing story, but he's also in pursuit of something murkier: the double-edged nature of doing good in a land where 'the past has only just happened.'" —*The New Yorker*

THE
GOOD
DOCTOR

THE
GOOD
DOCTOR

DAMON GALGUT

Grove Press
New York

First published in Great Britain in 2003 by Atlantic Books, an imprint of Grove Atlantic Ltd.

Printed in the United States of America

Library of Congress Cataloging-in-Publication Data
Galgut, Damon, 1963–
The good doctor / Damon Galgut.
p. cm.
ISBN 978-0-8021-4169-9
eISBN 978-0-8021-9149-6
1. Rural hospitals—Fiction. 2. South Africa—Fiction.
3. Physicians—Fiction. 4. Smuggling—Fiction.
5. Betrayal—Fiction. I. Title.
PR9369.3.G28G66 2004
811'.54—dc22   2003060150

Grove Press
an imprint of Grove Atlantic
154 West 14th Street
New York, NY 10011

Distributed by Publishers Group West

groveatlantic.com

Hundreds of miles of desolate, monotonous, burnt-up steppe cannot induce such deep depression as one man when he sits and talks, and one does not know when he will go.

CHEKHOV

Acknowledgements

I am grateful to the National Arts Council of South Africa for supporting me as writer-in-residence at the University of Cape Town during the latter half of 1998.

Many thanks are also due to my agent Tony Peake for his honest eye and unwavering support; to Lyn Denny for helping me with a few stray facts; to Alison Lowry and Clara Farmer for their editorial input; and to Riyaz Ahmad Mir for keeping me company.

Author's Note

The homelands of South Africa were impoverished and underdeveloped areas of land set aside by the apartheid government for the 'self-determination' of its various black 'nations'.

THE
GOOD
DOCTOR

1

The first time I saw him I thought, *he won't last.*

I was sitting in the office in the late afternoon and he appeared suddenly in the doorway, carrying a suitcase in one hand and wearing plain clothes—jeans and a brown shirt—with his white coat on top. He looked young and lost and a bit bewildered, but that wasn't why I thought what I did. It was because of something else, something I could see in his face.

He said, 'Hello . . . ? Is this the hospital?'

His voice was unexpectedly deep for somebody so tall and thin.

'Come in,' I said. 'Put down your bag.'

He came in, but he didn't put down the bag. He held it close while he looked around at the pink walls, the empty chairs, the dusty desk in the corner, the frail plants wilting in their pots. I could see that he thought there'd been some kind of mistake. I felt sorry for him.

'I'm Frank Eloff,' I said.

'I'm Laurence Waters.'

'I know.'

'You know . . . ?'

He seemed amazed that we should be expecting him, though he'd been sending faxes for days already, announcing his arrival.

'We're sharing a room,' I told him. 'Let me take you over.'

The room was in a separate wing. We had to cross an open space of ground, close to the parking lot. When he came in he must have walked this way, but now he looked at the path through the long grass, the ragged trees overhead dropping their burden of leaves, as if he'd never seen them before.

We went down the long passage to the room. I'd lived and slept alone in here until today. Two beds, a cupboard, a small carpet, a print on one wall, a mirror, a green sofa, a low coffee table made of synthetic wood, a lamp. It was all basic standard issue. The few occupied rooms all looked the same, as in some featureless bleak hotel. The only trace of individuality was in the configuration of the furniture, but I'd never bothered to shift mine around till two days ago, when an extra bed had been brought in. I also hadn't added anything. There was no personality in the ugly, austere furniture; against this neutral backdrop, even a piece of cloth would have been revealing.

'You can take that bed,' I said. 'There's space in the cupboard. The bathroom's through that door.'

'Oh. Yes. Okay.' But he still didn't put down his bag.

I'd only heard two weeks before that I would have to share a room. Dr Ngema had called me in. I wasn't happy, but I didn't refuse. And in the days that followed I came around, in spite of myself, to the idea of sharing. It might not be so bad. We might get on well, it might be good to have company, my life here could be pleasantly different. So in a way I started looking forward with curiosity to this change. And before he arrived I did a few things to make him welcome. I put the new bed under the window and made it up with fresh linen. I cleared a few shelves in the cupboard. I swept and cleaned, which is something I don't do very often.

But now that he was standing here I could see, through his eyes, how invisible that effort was. The room was ugly and bare. And Laurence Waters didn't look to me like the person I'd pictured in my head. I don't know what I'd imagined, but it wasn't this bland, biscuit-coloured young man, almost a boy still, who was at last putting his suitcase down.

He took his glasses off and rubbed them on his sleeve. He put them on again and said wearily, 'I don't understand.'

'What?'

'This whole place.'

'The hospital?'

'Not just the hospital. I mean . . .' He waved a hand to indicate the world out there. He meant the town outside the hospital walls.

'You asked to come here.'

'But I didn't know that it would be like this. Why?' he said with sudden intensity. 'I don't understand.'

'We can talk about it later. But I'm on duty now, I have to go back to the office.'

'I must see Dr Ngema,' he said abruptly. 'She's expecting me.'

'Don't worry about that now. You can do it in the morning. No hurry.'

'What should I do now?'

'Whatever you like. Unpack, settle in. Or come and sit with me. I'll be finished in a couple of hours.'

I left him alone and went back. He was shocked and depressed. I understood that; I'd felt it myself when I first arrived. You came expecting one thing and were met by something else completely.

You came expecting a busy modern hospital—rural maybe, and small, but full of activity—in a town where things were happening. This was the capital of what used to be one of the homelands, so whatever the morality of the politics that gave rise to it, you expected a place full of administration and movement, people coming and going. And when you'd turned off the main route to the border and were coming in on the one minor road that led here, it might still look—when you saw the place from a distance—like what you'd expected. There was the main street, leading to the centre where the fountain and the statue stood, the shop-fronts and pavements and streetlights, and all the buildings beyond. It looked neat and calibrated and exact. Not a bad place to be.

And then you arrived and you saw. Maybe the first clue was a disturbing detail; a crack that ran through an otherwise pristine wall, or a set of broken windows in an office you passed. Or the fact that the fountain was dry and full of old sand at the bottom. And you slowed down, looking around you with vague anxiety, and suddenly it all came into clear focus. The weeds in the joints of the pavements and bricks, the grass growing at places in the street, the fused lamps and the empty shops behind their blank glass fronts and the mildew and damp and blistered paint and the marks of rain on every surface and the slow tumbling down of solid structures, sometimes grain by grain, sometimes in pieces. And you were not sure any more of where you were.

And there were no people. That was the last thing you noticed, though you realized then that it was the first thing to give you that uneasy hollow feeling: the place was deserted. There was, yes, a car cruising slowly down a back road, an official uniform or two ambling along a pavement, and maybe a figure slouching on a footpath through an overgrown plot of land, but mostly the space was empty. Uninhabited. No human chaos, no movement.

A ghost town.

'It's like something terrible happened here,' Laurence said. 'That's how it feels.'

'*Ja,* but the opposite is true. Nothing has ever happened here. Nothing ever will. That's the problem.'

'But then how . . . ?'

'How what?'

'Nothing. Just how.'

He meant, *how did it come to be here at all*? And that was the real question. This was not a town that had sprung up naturally for the normal human reasons—a river in a dry area, say, or a discovery of gold, some kind of historical event. It was a town that had been conceived and planned on paper, by evil bureaucrats in a city far away, who had probably never even been here. Here is our homeland, they said, tracing an outline on a map, now where should its capital be? Why not here, in the middle? They made an 'X' with a red pen and all felt very satisfied with themselves, then sent for the state architects to draw up plans.

So the bewilderment that Laurence Waters felt wasn't unusual. I'd been through it myself. And so I knew that the feeling would pass. In a week or two the bewilderment would give way to something else: frustration maybe, or resentment, anger. And then that would turn into resignation. And after a couple of months Laurence would be suffering through his sentence here, like the rest of us, or else plotting a way to get out.

'But where are they all?' he said, talking more to the ceiling than to me.

'Who?'

'The people.'

'Out there,' I said. 'Where they live.'

This was hours later in my room—our room—that night. I had just put out the light and was lying there, trying to sleep, when his voice came out of the dark.

'But why do they live out there? Why aren't they here?'

'What's there for them here?' I said.

'Everything. I saw the countryside when I was driving. There's nothing out there. No hotels, shops, restaurants, cinemas . . . Nothing.'

'They don't need all that.'

'What about the hospital? Don't they need that?'

I sat up on one elbow. He was smoking a cigarette and I could see the red glow rising and falling. He was on his back, looking up.

'Laurence,' I said. 'Understand one thing. This isn't a real hospital. It's a joke. When you were driving here, do you remember the last town you passed, an hour back? That's where the real hospital is. That's where people go when they're sick. They don't come here. There's nothing here. You're in the wrong place.'

'I don't believe that.'

'You'd better believe it.'

The red coal hung still for a moment, then rose and fell, rose and fell. 'But people get injured, people get sick. Don't they need help?'

'What do you think this place means to them? It's where the army came from. It's where their puppet dictator lived. They hate this place.'

'You mean politics,' he said. 'But that's all past now. It doesn't matter any more.'

'The past has only just happened. It's not past yet.'

'I don't care about that. I'm a doctor.'

I lay and watched him for a while. After a few minutes he stubbed out the cigarette on the windowsill and threw the butt out of the window. Then he said one or two words I couldn't hear, made a gesture with his hands and sighed and went to sleep. It was almost instantaneous. He went limp and I could hear the regular sound of his breathing.

But I couldn't sleep. It had been years and years since I'd had to spend a night in the same room with anybody else. And I remembered then—almost incongruously, because he was nothing to me—how there had been a time, long before, when the idea of having somebody sleeping close to me in the dark was a consolation and comfort. I couldn't think of anything better. And now this other breathing body made me tense and watchful and somehow angry, so that it took hours before I was tired enough to close my eyes.

2

For a long time now there had only been the seven of us: Tehogo and the kitchen staff, Dr Ngema, the Santanders and me. Once upon a time it was different. There had been an Indian woman doctor when I first arrived, but she was long gone, and a white man from Cape Town who'd got married later and emigrated. There had been four or five nurses too, but they'd been retrenched or transferred, all except Tehogo. There were too many of us to deal with the tiny trickle of human need. So when somebody went away they were never replaced, the empty space they left behind immediately sandbagged and fortified as a bastion against final collapse.

So Laurence's arrival was a mysterious event. It made no sense. When Dr Ngema told me there was a young doctor coming to do a year of community service, I thought at first that she was making a joke. I had heard about the community service—it was a new government scheme, aimed at staffing and servicing all the hospitals in the country. But we seemed too obscure to qualify.

'Why?' I said. 'We don't need anybody else.'

'I know,' she said. 'I didn't request anybody. He asked to come here.'

'He asked? But why?'

'I don't know.' She was looking in perplexity at a letter that had been faxed to her. 'We don't have a choice, Frank. We have to find a place for him.'

'Well, all right,' I said, shrugging. 'It doesn't affect me.'

Dr Ngema looked up and sighed. 'It does affect you, I'm afraid,' she said. 'I have to put him into the room with you.'

'What?'

Nothing like this had ever happened before. She saw the dismay in my face.

'It won't be for long, Frank. When the Santanders go I'll put him in there.'

'But . . . we have a whole passage full of empty rooms. Why can't he go into one of those?'

'Because there's no furniture in those rooms. The only thing I can provide is a bed. But what about tables, chairs . . . ? He's got to sit somewhere. Please, Frank. I know it's hard. But somebody has to compromise.'

'But why me?'

'Who else, Frank?'

This wasn't a simple question. But there was one other room, down at the end of the passage, that was under dispute.

'Tehogo,' I said.

'Frank. You know that's not possible.'

'Why not?'

She shifted uncomfortably in her chair and her voice rose a note or two in protest. 'Frank. Frank. What can I do? Please. I will sort something out, I promise you. But I can't just evict him.'

'You don't have to evict him. Why can't they share?'

'Because . . . Tehogo isn't a doctor, you are. It makes sense for two doctors to share.'

Behind the words were other words, not spoken. It wasn't just that Laurence Waters and I were doctors; it was that we were two white men, and we belonged in a room together.

When the alarm woke me in the morning he was already up and dressed, sitting on the edge of his bed, smoking a cigarette.

'I want to meet Dr Ngema,' he said immediately.

'You can. But you'll have to wait a bit.'

'I could go over to her office. You don't have to take me. I could go on my own.'

'It's six in the morning, she isn't there yet. Relax, goddamn it, calm down. Have a shower or something.'

'I've already had one.'

When I went into the bathroom, the floor was swimming with water and he'd slung his damp towel over the door. There were bristles and shaving foam in the basin. My mood dropped as I cleaned up behind him, and it dropped even more when I came out again into the blue haze of his cigarette smoke. He was walking around aimlessly, puffing and thinking. When I coughed he stubbed the cigarette out on the windowsill, just as he'd done last night, and threw it away.

'You can't keep doing that. You're making burn marks everywhere.'

'There isn't an ashtray. I looked.'

'I don't smoke. You'll have to buy one.'

'It's a dirty habit, I know, I must give up.' He cast around him in a feverish way, then subsided on to the bed. 'Are you ready to go?'

'I have to get dressed, Laurence. Why are you in such a hurry? There's nothing to rush for.'

'Really?'

I dressed slowly, watching him. His attention settled on me only every few seconds, then flitted off to some arbitrary detail, sometimes outside the window. He seemed pent-up and distracted for no reason that I could see. It was a quality I would come to know well in him, but on that first day it was peculiar and disturbing.

Finally I was ready. 'All right,' I said. 'We can go. But, Laurence . . . your white coat. We don't really wear them here.'

He hesitated for a second, but he didn't take it off. I locked up and we went along the footpath under the heavy leaves, the light getting stronger all around. I could feel him edging towards the main block, to the office and officialdom, but I took him on a side path, to where we had breakfast. The dining room was in a third building of the hospital, along with the kitchen and the quarters for the cooking and cleaning staff, which were almost deserted by now. It was a long hall, half of which was used as a recreation room, the other half taken up by a big rectangular table, covered with a dirty cloth.

I introduced Laurence to the Santanders, Jorge and Claudia; they looked at him in startled surprise.

'You are . . . new?' Jorge said.

'Yes, community service. One year.'

'Excuse,' Claudia said, 'what service you say?'

'It's a government plan,' I said. 'All new doctors have to do it. After they've qualified.'

'Ah. Ah.' But they looked at him in bemusement. They had seen a few people leave this place, but he was the first one to arrive.

A silence fell. There was always an awkwardness around me and the Santanders, but it was deepened today by Laurence, who fidgeted his way through breakfast, pushing his toast around the plate, not really eating. He made a few desultory attempts at conversation and then none of us talked any more; there was only the scraping of metal spoons on plates and laughter from the kitchen next door, before they excused themselves and left.

Then it was just him and me, staring at the other half of the long room, with its clutter of ping-pong table and black-and-white television and old magazines and boxes of games.

I think it had started to dawn on him what sort of a place this was. There was no trace left of the manic urgency from the bedroom. When he'd finished eating he lit another cigarette, but he hardly puffed at it, just sat gazing into the distance while the smoke unravelled from his fingers.

Later we went over to the main building together. There was nobody in the office, although Claudia Santander was still officially on duty and Tehogo was supposed to be around. While we waited for Dr Ngema to appear, we sat and drank coffee in silence. Years of my life, sour with caffeine, had been sipped away in this room. A clock on the wall stood silent and broken, the hands fixed for ever at ten to three. The only thing that had changed here since I arrived was the dartboard on the back of the door. I had brought it up from the recreation room one Sunday, hoping to while away some hours. But there are only so many times that you can throw a dart into a board before the idea of an aim and a target begins to lose its point.

Dr Ngema arrived punctually at nine. She was here for ward rounds. This was a daily routine, even on those days—which is to say most of the time—when there were no patients in the hospital. There was always something to discuss, however inconsequential or arbitrary, some point of protocol or procedure. But today, as it happened, there were two patients to attend to.

She stopped in the doorway and her eyes went sideways to the anomalous brightness of Laurence's white coat. He had stood up and was smiling, holding out his hand.

'I'm Laurence Waters,' he said.

She shook his hand in confusion. 'Oh, yes,' she said, 'yes. When did you arrive?'

'Yesterday. Last night. I wanted to come and see you then, but Frank said . . .'

'I thought it would be too late,' I said. 'I told him to wait till today.'

'Yes,' Dr Ngema said. 'Yes.' She nodded vigorously.

A silence fell. Laurence was standing there with a broad and expectant smile, eyes shining, and it was obvious that he thought something would finally happen. All the rest—his arrival, waiting, talking to me—was just preparation. He had met the boss now, and a life of duty and meaning would be given to him.

But Dr Ngema was looking around, frowning. 'Where is Tehogo?' she said.

'I don't know. He hasn't arrived yet.'

'Oh. Well. Yes . . . Shall we go?'

I walked next to her, while Laurence followed behind. Our footsteps echoed importantly in all the emptiness. Both the patients were in the first ward, the only one that was really functioning. This was two doors up the passage from the office. The first room you passed, on the left, was the surgery, where examinations and any kind of operating were done. That door was closed. The next one you came to, on the right, was the ward. It looked like a normal room in a normal hospital. Two rows of beds, curtains, a dim fluorescent glow.

We all congregated around the bed of the first patient, a young man in his early twenties who had come into the country illegally on foot. Because we were close to the border we got a lot of these cases: people who had walked great distances without money or food. The border crossing was dangerous. This young man had made it through, but he was badly sunburned and dehydrated and his feet were raw. He was being intravenously rehydrated, and seemed to be making good progress. He didn't communicate with us, except by frightened glarings of his eyes.

'His blood pressure is 130 over 80. When did Tehogo do this chart?'

'I have no idea.'

'He must write in the time. He must do it clearly. Will you tell him? Frank, his temperature's a bit high. But he's passing urine again. What do you think?'

'Try him again with solid foods in the morning.'

'I agree. Will you pass that on to Tehogo as well?'

'Okay.'

'When do you think he can be discharged?'

'He's making good progress,' I said. 'Day after tomorrow.'

Dr Ngema nodded. We weren't friends; she didn't have any friends, but she always made a public point of asking my opinion. We had what is known as 'a good working relationship'.

We crossed over now to the other patient, a woman who'd been brought in by her husband a couple of days before in a lot of pain. It was her appendix, about to burst, and Dr Ngema had operated immediately. Appendicitis was the sort of emergency we liked: recognizable and treatable, within the scope of our resources.

Most surgery in the hospital was carried out by Dr Ngema, though her hand was far from steady, and in my opinion she had an unreliable eye. For personal reasons I was keen to build up some kind of record with surgery, but I was only allowed to do occasional minor procedures. It rankled with me, but I couldn't afford to let any resentment show. I had swallowed a lot of frustration over the years.

This morning, for example. I could see very quickly that all wasn't well with this patient—she was weak, and a brief examination showed some distension of her abdomen—but this wasn't the time or place to be too direct. Dr Ngema was sensitive to criticism, but there was more to it than that. If anything was wrong we would have to send the patient to that big hospital in the nearest town, an hour away, where there were more sophisticated supplies and staff. In extreme cases, where we could do nothing more, we were obliged to pass the patients on, but this was always a last resort, because every failure on our part made it harder to justify the thin funding we still had.

'Why don't we keep an eye on her?' I said. 'We can monitor it.'

Dr Ngema nodded slowly. 'All right.'

'It's leaking,' Laurence said.

We both looked at him.

'The stump is leaking,' he said. 'Look. Distended abdomen. Painful to pressure. You can't leave it too long.'

The silence that followed was filled with the hoarse breathing of the woman in the bed.

'Laurence,' I said.

I had spoken sharply, to put him in his place, but there was nothing to follow on his name. He was right: we both knew it, and the simple fact of his statement was obvious enough to shame us.

'Yes,' Dr Ngema said. 'Yes. We can all see that, I think.'

'What would you like me to do?' I asked quickly.

'Take her this morning. I'll stand by for you, Frank, while you're gone. It's better that we . . . yes. Yes. Let's do it.'

She was talking calmly and carefully, but it wasn't a happy moment. When she turned abruptly and walked back to the office I
didn't take up my usual place next to her, but lagged behind, a pace
out of step. Laurence jumped in next to her.

'Dr Ngema,' he said. 'Could I talk to you for a moment? I want
to know what's expected of me.'

'What do you mean?'

'What are my duties?' he said cheerfully. 'I'm keen to get started,
you see.'

She didn't answer immediately, but at the office door she turned
to him. 'You ride along with Frank,' she said. 'You might learn
something.'

'Okay.'

'Yes,' she said. 'Frank is a very experienced doctor. You can learn
a lot . . . from experienced people.'

It was the sharpest I'd ever seen her, but he seemed oblivious. He
followed me like a puppy into the office, where Tehogo was sitting
at the desk, staring darkly at the grain in the wood.

'I'm taking that appendix patient to the other hospital,' I said.
'And Tehogo, you must write in the time on the chart. The other
patient, the young man, can have solid food from tomorrow.'

'Yes,' Tehogo said, not looking up. He managed to make it sound
as though he was granting permission. Nothing punctured his dour
composure, not even surprise, but he did look startled for a moment
when my new room-mate sprang at him, hand extended.

'Hello,' he said. 'Pleased to meet you. My name's Laurence
Waters.'

I busied myself with routine and it was late morning already when
we set out. The hospital owned one antiquated ambulance, though
the official driver had long ago departed; whenever the ambulance was sent out, one of the doctors had to drive it. We put the
woman into the back on a stretcher and I got into the driver's seat.

I expected Laurence to sit up in the front with me, but he got into the back with the patient and crouched over her with intense attention, like an owl over its prey.

'Give her space to breathe,' I said. 'You'll make her feel claustrophobic.'

'Sorry. Sorry.' He pulled back, looking abashed, and I studied his broad face in the mirror. He seemed to wear a perpetual frown, as if one eternal question continually niggled at him.

I didn't speak to him while I warmed the engine and then pulled out into the street. The town, with all its vacant, impressive space, passed slowly by. Then we were on the tributary road that led to the main road, and the bush pressed in on either side. Heat made the leaves blurred, like a solid wall you couldn't penetrate. The road wandered between ridges and low hills. It was a hot, dense country, growing between extremes of brown grass and the brilliant green of riverine bush.

When I first got here I loved the landscape, the fertility and fecundity of it, the life it gave off. There were no bare places. Everything was shrouded in shoots and thorns and leaves; there were little paths running everywhere, made by animals or insects. The smells and colours were powerful. I used all my free time, hours and hours of it, to go off walking into the bush. I wanted to move closer to the lush heart of things. But over time what had compelled me most deeply began to show a different, hidden side. The vitality and heat became oppressive and somehow threatening. Nothing could be maintained here, nothing stayed the same. Metal started to corrode and rust, fabrics rotted, bright paint faded away. You could not clear a place in the forest and expect to find it again two weeks later.

When we got to the main road, the countryside changed around us: the bush was thinner here, there were more human settlements. Villages appeared on either side—congregations of huts, roofed conically in thatch and painted with bright designs. The ground was tramped hard and flat with use. The eyes of children or toiling men or idle old people watched us pass. Women stood up from scrappy fields of vegetables, hoe in hand.

After half an hour we reached the escarpment, where the road lifted and climbed. This marked the edge of what had used to be the homeland, and the beginning of viable industry: the land was dark with pine trees, planted in rows. From the top there was a brief view of the plain we'd left behind, an undulating sheet of mildewed bronze, before the grasslands started.

The town that we were going to, with its busy hospital, wasn't far on the other side of the escarpment: a turn-off, a short side road, and we were there. Even in the midday heat, when the surrounding streets were torpid and sun-struck, there was a quiet commotion of activity around the hospital entrance—cars and people coming and going. Although the patient wasn't quite an emergency case I delivered her to the emergency section. There was a doctor I'd often dealt with, a cocky young man not much older than Laurence, called du Toit. He was working today; I'd spoken to him earlier on the phone. He'd got all the forms ready to be signed and came to meet me with an insolent grin.

'Another one for us to take over,' he said. 'What's the matter, haven't you managed to kill her properly yet?'

'I thought I'd leave it to you.'

'Any time you want a real job, you know where to come. How long are you going to keep yourself buried in the backwoods down there?'

'As long as it takes,' I said, signing my name for the hundredth time on the same official form, watching the woman being wheeled away. Every time I came to make a delivery there was a variation on this dark exchange of banter between du Toit and me.

He was looking at Laurence with interest. 'You're new,' he said. 'I thought they were getting rid of people, not taking them on.'

'I'm here for community service,' Laurence said. 'One year.'

Du Toit snorted. 'Bad luck. You drew the short straw, hey?'

'No, no. I wanted to come.'

'Sure. Sure. Don't worry, it'll be over soon.' He slapped Laurence on the shoulder and said to me, 'Want some lunch?'

'Got to go back, thanks. I'm on duty. Next time.'

When we were outside again Laurence said, 'I don't like him.'

'He's all right.'

'He's spoilt. He's full of himself. He's not a real doctor, you can see that.'

Near the top of the escarpment I pulled over at a roadside restaurant I knew.

'What now?' Laurence said.

'I'm stopping for some lunch. Aren't you hungry?'

'I thought we were on duty. You see,' he said knowingly, 'you didn't want to have lunch with that guy. You don't like him much either.'

We sat at a table and had our lunch while we watched the other customers come and go. Most of the traffic on this road consisted of trucks on their way to and from the border, and the drivers often stopped here to eat and drink. I liked the look of these men. They had none of the harried introspection that doctors carried around with them. Their lives unravelled in the long lines of the road.

'So that's it,' Laurence said suddenly. 'The other hospital. The one where everybody goes.'

I nodded heavily. 'That's it.'

'That's where all the funding's going, the equipment, the staff, all that?'

'That's it.'

'But why?'

'Why? An accident of history. A few years ago there was a line on a map, somewhere around where we're sitting now. On one side was the homeland where everything was a token imitation. On the other side was the white dream, where all the money—'

'Yes, yes, I understand that,' he said impatiently. 'But the line on the map's gone now. So why aren't we the same as them?'

I shrugged. 'I don't know, Laurence. There isn't enough money to go round. They have to prioritize.'

'They're high priority, we're nothing.'

'That's about it. They'd like to close us down.'

'But. But.' The frown on his forehead was deep and vexed. 'That's all politics again, isn't it.'

'Everything is politics, Laurence. The moment you put two people in a room together, politics enters in. That's how it is.'

This thought seemed to quieten him; he didn't talk again until we were leaving. Then he suddenly announced that he wanted to drive.

'What?'

'I feel like it. Come on, Frank, let me have a turn. I want to see how it feels.'

I threw the keys to him. Before we were out of the parking lot I could feel what a careful driver he was, slow and controlled, quite contrary to the feverish way he talked and behaved. But this was just one of the contradictions in Laurence, the little flaws and gaps that didn't add up.

It was the middle of the afternoon by now. The bottom of the escarpment was dark with shadow; when we broke out into sun again the shadows of objects were stretched long and narrow on the ground. The road went straight as a dart towards the horizon and the border. After twenty minutes of driving I said to him, 'Pull over.'

The impulse seemed to come from nowhere, but I realized now that it had been rising in me all day, from early that morning. Even maybe from before.

'Hey?'

'Here, by the trees.'

There was a small clump of bluegums at the edge of the road, with a tiny wooden shack set a little way back. Behind that again, over the top of a small rise, the roofs of a village were just visible.

'But what for?'

'Let's just take a look.'

Then he saw the sign and read it aloud. '"Souvenirs and handicrafts".'

'Let's see what they've got.'

There was another car parked outside the door. An American couple, loud and studiously friendly, was leaving, carrying two carved wooden giraffes. Behind them the woman who ran this little informal shop was standing at the door, smiling. When she saw me the smile vanished, then came tightly back again.

To the Americans she called, 'Have a good holiday.'

She was in her early thirties. Small-boned but strong, with a wide, open face. Barefoot, in a ragged red dress.

We went past her into the dim inside of the shack. There were rough shelves carrying handicrafts—animal figures carved out of wood, beadwork, woven mats and baskets, toys made out of wire. Potted Africa, endlessly replicated and served up for the tourists. A hand-painted sign full of misspellings told us that this work was made by people from all the villages in the district. We wandered around, looking over the shelves. It was very hot in there.

Laurence said, 'It's so . . .'

'So what?'

'So poor.'

The car drove off outside and she came back in, rubbing her arms. 'Hello, how are you?' she said, speaking to nobody in particular.

'Okay,' I said. 'And you?'

'You want to buy something?'

'We're just having a look.'

Laurence was staring around with a pained expression. 'Is this your shop?' he said.

'No. I'm just working here.'

'Who does it belong to?'

She waved a hand at the door. Someone out there.

'Very nice.'

She smiled and nodded. 'Yes, yes,' she said. 'Welcome.'

'I'm going to get something for you, Frank,' he said. He held up a crude wooden carving of a fish.

'Twenty-five rand,' she told him.

'To thank you for taking me around today. I've had a very good time.'

'That's all right. You don't have to do that. It's all right.'

'I want to.'

'Twenty,' she said.

'I'm giving you twenty-five.' He counted the money into her hand. 'Thank you. You have a very nice shop. What is your name?'

'Maria.'

'You have a nice shop, Maria.'

'I think so too,' I said.

She looked directly at me then, for the first time since I'd come in, and said, 'You have been too much busy.'

It wasn't a question, but I answered as if it was. 'Um, *ja, ja,* I have.'

I held the blunt shape of the fish in my lap as we drove out of the bluegums. Against the late light the escarpment was a dark wave, poised to break.

'You've been there before,' he said.

'Yes, I stopped on my first day. On my way to the hospital.'

'But that was years ago.'

'Yes.'

He rolled down his window and the warm air went over us. We were speeding through the end of the afternoon and it felt as if all the places we'd visited today were strewn haphazardly behind us, like points on a map that only we could read. It had been a good day, weightless somehow, so it came with the heaviness of a blow when he suddenly asked in a conversational voice, 'Have you slept with that woman?'

'What?'

'That woman in the shop. Have you—'

'Yes, I heard you. No. No. What gave you that idea?'

'I don't know, something in the air.'

'Well, I haven't.'

'Are you offended?'

'No, I'm just . . . surprised.'

'Sorry. When I think something I just say it. I can't help it.'

We didn't speak again for the rest of the drive. It was almost twilight by the time we got back—the whole day gone, the end of my shift of duty. I didn't return to the office, but I didn't want to sit in the room either. There was nothing to do and I felt restless, uncontained.

Laurence didn't want to go for supper, he said he wasn't hungry, so I went alone to the dining room. But I wasn't hungry either, and I found myself sitting in the recreation room in front of the television, the sound turned off, empty images flickering, throwing a table-tennis ball from hand to hand. A discontent was stirring in me. Old questions I had learned not to ask were back with me again. Old yearnings and needs. It was hard to sit still and after an hour or two I dropped the ball and let it roll. I went out to the car park. The light in my room was on, but it was turned off suddenly as I watched.

I drove slowly at first, but then with gathering speed. It felt as if I had a mission to be discharged with urgency and purpose, when the truth was all aimlessness, unease. I parked in the usual place and walked back to the shack. She'd heard the car and was waiting for me. She took me by the hand and led me in and turned her back briefly while she latched the door—a lock a child could break, a piece of string wound on a nail.

3

I hadn't lied about everything to Laurence: I did stop at the little shack that first day on my way to the town. I was looking at things; this was one more thing to look at. And Maria was there. Wearing that same red dress, maybe, her feet bare. She said hello as I cast my dazed eye over the shelves of carved animals.

'You want elephant,' she said.

'No, no, I'm just looking.'

'Looking is free.'

'Yes,' I said.

Or maybe none of this was said, maybe her dress was black. I don't remember any of it. I don't even have an image of her face from that first day; I only know that I went there and that I certainly saw her, because the next time I went back some old recognition stirred in me. And she knew me immediately; she smiled and asked me how I was.

This was almost two years later. I was driving back from taking a patient to that other, better hospital, and I saw the sign tied to a tree next to the road. It was something about the sign—the pathos of the rough lettering, the misspelling—that made me stop.

Then her face, the wide smile. 'How are you today?' she said. 'You are not sad?'

'Not sad?'

'Last time you are too much sad.'

She was wearing a dark blue cotton dress that had been rubbed down almost to transparency in places. Her wrists and ankles were heavy with beads.

'What's your name?'

'I am Maria.'

'No, what's your real name? Your African name.'

But something closed over in her face; she dropped her eyes. 'Maria,' she repeated. 'Maria.'

I left it like that. The name was wrong on her, it didn't fit into her mouth, but I liked the demure determination with which she'd set up this little barrier. She seemed suddenly mysterious to me.

I sat on a wooden crate in the corner for maybe two hours, talking to her. It wasn't a conversation; I was asking her questions and she answered. *Who are you? Where do you come from? How old are you?* I wanted to know everything.

She'd been working there for three years. She did everything in the tiny shack—ate, slept, washed. When I asked her where all her things were she pointed to a battered suitcase of clothes under one of the shelves. She showed me her bed: a ragged blanket, folded up neatly into a square. A rusty bucket in the corner was her bath. She got water, she said, from the village just behind. Somebody there also came to bring food for her.

Was it her village? No, it wasn't. Her place was far from here. Why did she live here? Because of the shop. But why was the shop here? Because her husband built it here. It was his idea, he had brought her to work. It was he who got all the curios and carvings from the other villages and brought them here for her to sell. Did he stay with her in the shop? No, somewhere else. In the village at the back? No, in some other place, she was not sure where. He came sometimes, sometimes. When did she last see him? She held up six fingers. Hours, days, weeks?

She talked in half-words and mime, smiling the whole time. Once or twice she laughed at herself. I couldn't take my eyes off her. I was fascinated by this language of signals and signs, with its obscure calligraphy of gestures, that seemed to have been invented by us alone. I had never been anywhere before that was like this tiny square of sand with its shelves of wooden animals. Long before it got too dark in there to see properly I had the impulse to do what I eventually did: lean over and touch my fingers to her neck. She went very still.

'Come with me,' I said. 'Let's go somewhere.'

'Where?'

'My room.' I felt reckless.

She shook her head and pulled away from my hand.

'Why not?'

'Not possible,' she said. 'Not possible.'

I had gone too far; she was tense and distant with me now; I had read the whole situation wrongly. But when I had gathered myself together and stood up to leave, she said suddenly:

'Later.'

'Later?'

'You come after. After, when the shop is . . .' She gestured to indicate *closed, shut down.*

'What time?'

'Eight. When it is dark.'

'All right,' I said. 'I'll come back later.'

I went back to the hospital and showered and shaved and changed my clothes. I was charged with a voltage of yearning and dread. The assignation seemed to have arisen from a place in me I'd never known till then. What did I want? Why was I doing this? It occurred to me that the whole thing could be a set-up; other people could be lying in wait; murder, abduction, blackmail ringed me round. I knew clearly that I should not go back.

But I went back. I was very afraid. She was waiting for me. She told me to move the car away from the shack, further down, behind a line of bushes. I walked back through darkness, my heart tolling like a bell. She was also frightened, looking around her, holding her breath. The lamp was out. She led me in by the hand, to a space of dead time in which memory has no hold.

It was always the same. The pattern that we laid down that first night was repeated, over and over, on the nights that followed—the furtive parking of the car, the walk back to the door where she was waiting. Then she tied the door closed behind us and we lay down on the ragged blanket on the ground.

The sex was quick and urgent, half-clothed, always with an element of fear. I didn't know what we were afraid of, till one night she gave it a name: I mustn't come tomorrow, she said.

'Why not?'

'Danger, danger.'

'What danger?'

'My husband.'

Obviously I had to conceal myself from him, for her sake. But something in her also gave me to understand that he might harm me. She didn't want to talk more about it. On the next night I drove past to look and there was a car parked outside. A white car, what make I didn't know. Parked outside the door, in full view.

From that night he registered as a presence, standing behind her somewhere, face unclear. I waited a week before I went back to her. I said, 'Is he really your husband?'

She nodded solemnly.

'But really?' I said. 'Isn't he just your boyfriend? Did you actually get married? Married?'

'Married,' she said, nodding vigorously. It was impossible to tell if she had understood the question.

She didn't wear a wedding ring, but that didn't mean anything. In a life as stripped-down and bare as hers, none of the usual things applied. She might anyway have married in some ceremony or ritual that didn't involve a ring. There was no way to know. I liked that; I liked not knowing much about her. This wasn't a relationship in any normal sense of the word. I had never in my life had anything like this wordless obsession, with so many meanings implied or

understood. Of course there had been other women since my marriage had crashed; I'd had a short affair with Claudia Santander at
the hospital, there were a couple of brief encounters in passing, but
none of those liaisons were as silent or so disturbingly powerful as
this. All I had to go on was what I came to there at night: the poor
inside of the shack, the hard dirt floor, the smell of her sweat—
sometimes vaguely repellent—when I opened her dress. And the
hot, blind embrace in the dark.

We weren't tender with each other. Or only sometimes, in particular ways. I touched her and stroked her, but she never touched me
like that. And we weren't allowed to kiss—when I tried she turned
her head sharply away and said, 'No, no.' I asked why, but it was
never explained, and the silence suited me. It suited me too that we
weren't able to talk in any real way. We came together for the pri-
mal, intimate act, while keeping a huge distance open between us.

Sometimes there was no sex. Sometimes it wasn't what I was
looking for. I just lay there with my face against her shoulder and
one hand under her dress, on her breast. When this happened
it was usually in silence, just the sound of breathing in the dark.
But then once she did speak to me, a long soft monologue in her
own language. I didn't understand a word, but her voice sketched
out a story on the inside of my eyelids, in which she and I were
somewhere else.

So for a while I had two lives: one that was empty and adrift,
in the hospital by day, and another that was illicit and intense, by
the side of the road at night. The one had nothing to do with the
other. For a long time she had no curiosity about who I was or
what I did. And when she finally asked, I found myself telling a
lie. I said I was an engineer for the government, here on contract
for two years. I told her I was doing some work at the hospital at
the moment, which was how I came to be driving the ambulance
sometimes. I said I was living in a municipal flat in town, and that
I had a wife in the city who often came up to visit me. I don't know

why I told these lies, except that I wanted to keep her away from my other, daytime life.

I needn't have bothered. She never showed the slightest interest in uncovering the other side of me; the town itself seemed to exist for her on a different planet somewhere. Only once did I ever see her there. I was driving down the main street one afternoon and I spotted her on the pavement, walking alone. I pretended I hadn't seen her and turned off at the next corner. She never mentioned it to me, and perhaps she hadn't seen me either, but for two days afterwards I felt full of guilt and betrayal.

But I went back; I always went back. Every night that I wasn't on duty, or when she hadn't asked me not to come, I found myself on the road when it got dark, driving to her. And the shack, the weakest and flimsiest of structures, was always, permanently, there.

Then the thing between us began to seem like something solid too, something with foundations and dimensions, something real. And I became afraid of it. I told myself: *this can't go on, it must stop.* I didn't want something for which I felt obliged and responsible. I didn't want something for which I might have to pay one day.

Then one night she asked me for money.

Everything changed in a moment.

It was a casual request, as I was leaving. I was getting dressed, tying up my shoelaces, and she said, 'I have to ask favour.'

'What's that?'

But I knew. And I realized then that I'd been waiting for this since the very first night.

'I've got big problem. My husband . . .' She went into a long story about him, which I didn't understand. Before she'd finished I said, 'All right, how much do you need?'

'I'm asking two hundred rand.'

'All right.'

'You give it?'

'Yes.'

'This is only for borrow.'

'That's all right,' I said. 'You can keep it.'

I said it carelessly. Both of us were talking in a careless, offhand way.

After that I gave her money from time to time. Sometimes she asked, sometimes I just gave. There was about these transactions a trace always of that first revelatory moment; we were travelling in a different landscape now. And it was only now that I felt how much of my life up there in the hospital had been based on what was happening in the shack. How much meaning had been generated there—though I understood none of it. The way that everything had been till then—the feeling of stupid innocence—was gone. I started to doubt everything. I had a lot of questions: that first night, when she'd told me to come back later, what was going on in her mind? All the times I'd come here, looking for comfort and relief, had she been looking for something else? Was money the motive all along?

And now I saw, I really saw, what was in front of me. The crude little dwelling, with its sand floor and its odd smells, wasn't just an exotic backdrop to a nightly escape from my life: it was where she actually, permanently lived. She was very poor; she had nothing. The coins and notes that I stuffed into her hand on my way out of the door were a symbol of a separation between us that couldn't be measured: it was a disjuncture between our very lives. Money couldn't close the gap; it was the gap. We knew nothing about each other.

Now I couldn't stop thinking. During the day I thought about that hour or two at night. There was no way any more to know what was true. I suspected everything she told me. Even whether she lived in the shack. Maybe she didn't; maybe she went off somewhere else after I'd gone. I'd never spent the night to be sure. And her husband—did he actually exist? I had never seen him, only that white car outside, which could've belonged to anybody. And if he did exist—that shadowy, faceless man—did he know about me? Was he the one manipulating all these little events from a distance? All the lies I'd told, so small and harmless, were like confirmations that she was doing the same. It was so easy; why not? And then her sighs and broken English and explanations with her hands—it started to feel like dissembling and untruth. Maybe she could understand me perfectly when I talked. Oh, there was an element of craziness to my thinking, I knew that. But my suspicion and mistrust were boundless; as big, in fact, as my own dishonesty.

I started going there in the daytime. I told myself it was the proper thing to do: to see her in a normal way, when the sun was up. But I was trying to spy on her life, to find out who she was. I didn't find anything out. I sat there on the wooden crate, often for long stretches of silence. Other people were always passing through. There were travellers or tourists going over the border or to the game farms near by, and they would stop and look over the shelves and sometimes buy something. And there was a woman who came from the village behind the shack, bringing food or tea in chipped enamel plates and mugs; the first time she saw me she went away quickly, looking scared, but Maria must have spoken to her, because after that she would always sit for a while, smiling shyly and watching me. But she could speak no English at all.

And then somehow it was finished. As with my marriage, there was no clear climactic moment; it was more like something inevitable in the situation and in us, which over time worked its way into events. My weird romance that belonged to night and silence had become an ordinary daytime affair, as real as my life.

So I stopped going. Maybe not overnight, but gradually. I went only once a week, then every fortnight, and then a month went past. And suddenly it was all behind me. I drove by from time to time without stopping, just to make sure the shack was still there. Once the white car was parked outside and I had my first true, genuine pang of jealousy. But I didn't go back. I told myself that I would do it one day. I would just let a little time pass, a few months, to wipe out what had gone wrong. And then I would go back in the old way, at night, without too much talking. And it would be like it was when we'd started. But the little while turned into a long stretch of time—a year, a year and a half, more. And I knew then that I would never go back.

Until the day I went past with Laurence Waters, and it was all somehow different, and one thing led to another.

4

The morning after Laurence arrived, Dr Ngema asked me to come to her office to talk. We sat in the low chairs in front of her desk, a sign that we were going to have an informal, personal chat.

Dr Ngema was in her early sixties, a dry dusty bird of a woman with a serious face. It was a measure of the relationship between us that, although we called each other by our first names in conversation, I still thought of her in my mind as Dr Ngema. She was the head of the hospital, my employer and superior, but a complex bit of history made me heir to the throne, and the politics between us were difficult and fragile.

When I first came up to the hospital it was to take over from Dr Ngema. The post had been advertised at a critical juncture in my life. My marriage had collapsed, I couldn't continue my practice, and I wanted everything to change. A move up here seemed like the opportunity I was looking for. And for a while it was all set to fall into place.

Dr Ngema was moving to a new position in the Department of Health, down in the city. She'd been working at the hospital for ten or eleven years, after spending most of her life overseas in exile. She didn't want to be stranded out here, on the edge of things, but for her it was a way of treading water, just for a while, till she could move closer to the centre. Now her moment had come. She had only to fill her position behind her, and I was her choice. There were—I discovered afterwards—only three other applicants. But the selection committee consisted solely of Dr Ngema, and she saw in me whatever it was she was looking for.

So it had all seemed good for a while. I made my move up here a month early, to learn the ropes from her. But a week or two after I arrived, the post, whatever it was that she'd been aiming for, became suddenly unavailable again. Something had shifted somewhere. And my new job was suddenly unavailable too.

I could have left. I was offered a payout and an apology, and I could have retreated to the shambles of my old life. But I decided to stay. According to Dr Ngema, it was only a matter of time before the post she wanted would open up again, and of course if I was working here I would still be first in line. I didn't believe her, but I chose to believe her. It wouldn't be for long, I told myself—a year or two, and then I would reconsider my future.

But the year or two had become six or seven, and I still hadn't moved. From time to time there had been further rumours, little bursts of excitement from Dr Ngema: it was happening at last, the job was about to be offered; but these flurries always subsided again into resignation and disappointment. It wasn't her fault, but all of this pulling and pushing had made even the most innocuous conversation between us feel charged and significant.

Today she wanted to talk about Laurence. What he'd done yesterday—showing her up in front of me with the appendix patient—had upset her. She wanted him out, but of course she wouldn't say it like that.

'I have a feeling he was looking for a different kind of hospital,' she said. 'The set-up here—it's too low-key for someone like him.'

'I agree,' I said.

'Why don't you take him around, Frank? Show him the whole place. Let him see what he's in for. Then if he wants to be transferred somewhere else, I'll see what I can do.'

'All right. No problem.'

'Of course he's welcome here. I'm not saying he isn't. The community service idea—I'm in favour. I'm all for innovation and change, you know that.'

'Oh, yes,' I said. 'I know.'

Innovation and change: it was one of her key phrases, a mantra she liked to repeat. But it was empty. Ruth Ngema would go to great lengths to avoid any innovation or change, because who knew what might follow on? But I was in tune with her today, I knew what she wanted, and she understood my feelings too.

'And if he goes, you can have your room back to yourself,' she said. 'It just seems easier for everybody.'

So I showed Laurence around. It was strange being a guide. I had been there so long that I looked at things without seeing them. But now it all came into focus, as if it was my first day. I walked him through the hospital. The life and activity of the place was all at one end of the main building; there was no need to go further. Doors led into deserted wards, rows of beds standing spectral and naked between green curtains hanging on rails. Upstairs were the offices. Dr Ngema occupied the first one, directly above the front entrance. We saw her at her desk as we passed, head bowed over papers, pen scratching; she looked up and smiled knowingly as we went by. Then one empty cubicle after another, bare even of the simplest furniture. All these rooms, waiting to receive people and industry and labour that had just never come.

Although the hospital was nearly ten years old by now, it had never been properly completed. Too many things had intervened. It had started as the project of the first chief minister of the homeland, but as soon as all the buildings had gone up there was the military coup and everything had been stalled and suspended. It took another two years for all of it to get moving again. But not long after that the white government finally gave in, down in the real centre of power, far away, and it was all left hanging again. Then the homeland had ceased to be a homeland, and with its reabsorption into the country the meaning and the future of the hospital became permanently unclear.

So it was a strange twilight place, halfway between nothing and somewhere. The little jumble of disconnected buildings, like all the structures in the town, was slowly falling into ruin. Grass had started growing on the roof. The pink walls—nobody knew why it had all been painted pink—had faded with the weather into a pale shade of orange. The grounds behind their high wall and gate were going to seed. At night most of the windows, regularly repeated behind bars, were dark.

For the few of us still remaining, life went on between twin poles of banality and violence. There were long periods of tedium when nothing happened, the place was empty. Then suddenly there would be a flurry, somebody arriving in the middle of the night, injured, bleeding. And we would try to do something to help. But the truth is that we were very limited in what we could do. We were low on equipment and supplies and money. Or perhaps it would be more accurate to say that certain things were unavailable, while others were stacked up in the cupboards. We had large supplies of certain drugs we rarely used, while deliveries of vital medicines were frozen because of some massive unpaid bill higher up in the system somewhere. Condoms, for example: we had shelf after shelf of them, we didn't know what to do with them, while basics like swabs, sterile gloves and X-ray paper were on perpetual order, but never came. We had an electronic ventilator and one or two other pieces of critical-care equipment, but there were frequent power cuts and we couldn't get the provincial government to repair our faulty emergency generator. It was not unknown for operations to happen on critically injured patients by torchlight.

In the other building, where we slept, the conditions were very bad. At the far end of the passage was a door that led into a wing that had been planned as an extension of the main building. There were more wards here, more offices; it was a mirror image, really, of the main wing. But it had been plundered. There were one or two metal bed-frames left, and here and there a tattered curtain hanging down. Everything else that was usable had been stripped. In the bathroom the sinks had been pulled out of the wall, the metal heads of the showers removed. Pipes dangled into empty air. In one or two rooms the windows had been broken and birds had come in to nest. The burbling of doves echoed weirdly in the stillness and white stars of shit were splattered on the floor.

Both of us went silent as we paced through this neglect and slow decay. When we got to the other end where the entrance, all boarded up and barred, was supposed to lead out into the parking lot, we stopped. There was a window looking out on the overgrown plot of land between us and the main building. The shadows of leaves moved on our faces.

'I suppose it's not what you expected,' I said.

'No.'

'You don't have to stay. If you asked for a transfer, I'm sure Dr Ngema—'

'Oh,' he said, surprised. 'But I want to stay.'

I looked at him. With my new eyes I saw him properly for the first time. He was long and tall and thin. Under a fringe of blond hair, his face was flat and open. It was a plain face, ordinary, except for the quality I had seen in the first glance, laid over it like a second skin. This quality made his face somehow remarkable, but I couldn't give it a name.

'Why did you come here?' I said.

'But you know why.'

'I mean, why here? You asked to come to this hospital. You specially requested it. Why?'

He took his spectacles off and rubbed them on his sleeve. His grey eyes blinked dimly as he looked out of the window. 'I heard it was a tiny place,' he said. 'I heard there were a lot of problems.'

'I don't understand. Surely those are logical reasons not to be here. Why would you want to do this to yourself?'

He didn't want to get into that. He put on his glasses and pointed away, out of the window, above the trees, to the highest hill at the edge of town. 'Look! What's that?'

'That used to be the Brigadier's house.'

'Who's the Brigadier?'

'Are you serious?'

'*Ja*. Should I know? Did he do something famous?'

'He overthrew the homeland government in a military coup.'

But the interest had switched off in his face; he was looking around him, frowning again.

'All this,' he said. 'Will it just go to waste? What's being done with it? Will it just stand here?'

'It'll be picked to pieces, if you ask me. It's being stripped and stolen. Look. You can see.'

'But that's terrible. Who's doing it?'

I shrugged. 'Anybody can get in. The door's not locked.'

It didn't seem that important to me, but he was transfixed by a real dismay. I could see him noticing all the bare, exposed places in the filthy passage: the missing skirting boards, the ripped-out light fittings, the raw dangling wires. He shook his head. 'What for? Where does it go?'

'There are lots of poor people out there. They can use anything.'

'But it's for them. The hospital. It's for them!'

'You go and tell them that.'

I thought he might burst into tears. His expression was locked on a quandary that he just couldn't resolve. I put a hand on his shoulder and said: 'Come on, let's get out of here. It's too depressing.'

'Why doesn't anybody do something?'

'But what should they do?'

We walked back through the strange mausoleum, leaving the prints of our feet in the dust. Pigeons flurried up at our approach. Outside, blinking in the hot sun, I said, 'That's it. That's the hospital.'

'There's nothing more?'

'Well, what about taking a drive? We could have a look at the town.'

*   *   *

He had a tiny blue Volkswagen Beetle, older and more beaten up than my car. And he didn't look out of place behind the wheel. Something came over him that was almost careless, so that he didn't resemble any more the earnest young doctor in a white coat. 'Where to, Frank?' he said. 'You tell me where to go.'

We went slowly down the main street, which was the one tarred road in town, past empty shops with empty shelves. Here and there a viable business did function: the small supermarket stood idle and almost deserted in the heat, a single bored cashier at a till. The security guard outside, fanning himself in slow motion with his cap, watched the car go past like a distant event on television. At the main intersection, presiding over the cracked and crumbling fountain and its oval of brown lawn, the statue held its resolute pose, one hand on a hip and the other pointing forward, into the future or the bushveld. The legs were turning green.

'That's the Brigadier again, if you're interested.'

'Where?'

'I'm talking about the statue.'

'Oh, I see.'

'I can tell you a story about that.'

But again the interest had faded in his face: the story of the statue belonged to a world he didn't live in. So I didn't tell him how, not long after I arrived in the town, I had gone for a walk into the countryside near by. I was full of directionless fury in those days, which took me on long, demented forays into the bush, carrying a backpack and a tent. I rarely knew where I was going and, beating my way through an overgrown ravine near the north edge of town one day, I had come upon a huge metal object half swallowed in the sand. It might have fallen from the sky. It was an old bust the size of a car, and only after I had cleared away a mess of vines and creepers did I recognize the face of the previous chief minister of the homeland. In this bronze version of himself he was wearing an expression of penetrating piety. That was before the military coup and the twenty-four charges of corruption and fraud that sent him running for his life.

It was only a few days afterwards that I realized the bust had used to stand on the plinth at the main intersection where the Brigadier's statue was now. I could imagine the mob of cheering soldiers tearing it down with axes and chains and crowbars. I don't know how they got it out there, into the middle of the gorge, but it resembled nothing so much as a severed iron head, the body of which must be lying somewhere close by. I didn't go back there again.

I showed Laurence the absurd dome of the parliament building, nailed shut and disused. I showed him the library, which had never been stocked with books. The school, which had never taught a lesson. The blocks of flats, government housing for all the workers who were going to come and run the offices and services that had been planned—and some workers did come for a while. But there was no work. And then the trouble started, and in the end they trickled away again, to the cities or back where they'd come from, except the few who could still be spotted here and there, lost in their own uniforms and all this useless space.

And then the road came to the other side of town and faded away, in a short distance, into nothing. The buildings suddenly stopped along a line. In front of us the bush took over again: brown wastes of grass, with anthills and thorn trees rising out of it. In the distance, a dark stripe of forest.

He sat behind the wheel, staring into the simmering heat. His face had some of the same dismay it had worn in the hospital. 'What shall we do now?' he said. I thought I could detect a note of desperation.

'Would you like a drink?'

'But where?'

'There is one place in town.'

'Really?'

He was glaring at me; perhaps he suspected a joke. But in fact Mama Mthembu's place was very pleasant, and always incongruously crowded. Every bored civil servant and off-duty worker headed straight for it. And today, when we were sitting in the little courtyard under the bougainvillaea, with the emptiness and isolation sealed away outside, we could have been anywhere, in any happy country town. The dirty plastic tables and the sad faces at the bar didn't matter; we were surrounded by voices and movement, the illusion of community.

Mama Mthembu herself was an enormously fat old lady, always wearing the same floral print dress and slip-slops, and the same gap-toothed smile. She had a lot to smile about: she ran the one flourishing business in town. When she'd started the place was a hotel, but for obvious reasons this side of things had failed dismally. The two floors of rooms stood as empty as the hospital, and the focus of activity had moved downstairs and out, to the courtyard and bar.

She came over now, sweating and smiling amiably, to wipe the table with a filthy cloth. 'How are you today, Mr Doctor?' In all the time I'd been here, and despite the fact that I'd stayed in her hotel for two weeks when I'd first arrived, she had never learned my name.

'I'm good, Mama. How about you?'

'The same, the same. Who is your friend?'

'His name is Laurence Waters. He's a new doctor at the hospital.'

'Welcome, welcome. I can get you a beer?'

When she'd gone he asked, 'Why do you call her Mama?'

'That's what everybody calls her.'

'But why?'

'I don't know. It's a term of affection or something. Respect. I don't know.'

He looked around at the other people in the courtyard and I could see him relax visibly. It was nice here in the half-sun, entwined in other conversations. When Mama had brought our beers and we'd both taken a long cold drink, he sighed and said: 'In the hospital, you asked me why I wanted to come here.'

'Yes.'

'I want to explain it to you. But I'm not sure if you'll understand. All the others, the students, I mean, they just wanted the most comfortable posting. None of them wanted to do it anyway, they were angry. But if they had to go, they wanted it to be convenient, you know, a good hospital, close to home. They didn't care about it.'

'And you?'

'I thought: let me be different to them. Let me find the tiniest place, the furthest away from anything. Let me make it hard on myself.'

'But why?'

'I don't want to be like the rest.' He studied me uneasily through his spectacles, then dropped his eyes. 'Why?' he said. 'Do you think I'm a fool?'

'No. But it's a big symbolic gesture. What do you achieve?'

He said carefully, 'I want to do work that means something.'

'But you do want to work,' I said. 'You've come to a place where that doesn't always happen.'

He thought about this for a long time, biting his lip. 'Is it always like this?' he said at last. 'I mean, it can't be.'

'Why not?'

'Then it can change.'

'How?'

'People change things,' he said. 'People make things, they can change them.'

'You're idealistic,' I said.

I wanted to say, *you're very young.* I wanted to tell him, *you won't last.*

'Yes,' he said, nodding happily; he didn't detect any criticism. He sipped his beer and became serious again. 'You know,' he said, 'I like you, Frank.'

I didn't answer, the declaration made me uncomfortable, but the truth was that I liked him too. The feeling wasn't based on anything except the few hours we'd spent in each other's company, but already I was finding it difficult to resent him completely.

Which, in another way, made me resent him more.

5

Right from the beginning, Laurence was like two separate people to me. On the one hand he was my shadow, waiting for me when I opened my eyes, following me to meals and work, an unwanted usurper crowding me in my own room. And on the other hand he was a companion and confidant, who leavened the flat days with feeling and talk.

So I was also two people in my dealings with him. There was the dark, angry Frank, who felt himself under siege. And there was a softer Frank too, who was grateful not to be alone.

The last time I'd shared a room with anybody was with Karen, my wife—but that wasn't the same sort of sharing. Male company: two beds in a confined space: it was like the army again. But there was no code of discipline imposed on us from outside; there weren't even any rules. It was just two different natures thrown into a box.

He was messy and untidy. His habits from the first day didn't change—the clothes left lying around, the water on the bathroom floor. I cleaned up behind him, but he didn't seem to notice. When I bought an ashtray from the supermarket and left it conspicuously on the table, he went on throwing his cigarettes out of the window. It drove me crazy.

But he was also orderly and controlled, in a different sort of way. He would suddenly take it into his head to sweep some arbitrary corner, or clean some piece of wall. Then he scrubbed and scoured with peculiar intensity until he was satisfied, and could lean back with a cigarette to relax, dropping ash on the carpet.

One day I came in to find him rearranging the furniture in the room. He'd dragged the coffee table and cupboard and lamp around into new positions. It didn't matter, it didn't affect anything, but I felt a flash of personal outrage, as if he'd violated my home.

'You mustn't get too settled in here,' I told him. 'This is just temporary.'

'How do you mean?'

'You're not going to be staying here for too long. Dr Ngema's putting you into the Santanders' room next door, when they go.'

'Oh,' he said, looking stunned. 'I didn't know.'

But the furniture stayed where it was, in the new arrangement, and in a few days it seemed natural and normal to me. Not long after that he replaced the curtains and put up a couple of posters on the wall. I felt that same flash of outrage again, but more dimly this time, less deep. And when he set up a little shrine to his girlfriend on the windowsill above his bed, I felt almost nothing at all.

There were a few photographs, showing a small black woman with short hair. Around the photographs he'd arranged a little pile of stones, a dried leaf and a bracelet. These things had some kind of personal significance for him.

'What's her name?'

'Zanele.'

'Where did you meet her?'

'In the Sudan.'

'The Sudan?'

He was pleased at how amazed I was. 'Sure. I spent a year after school travelling around Africa. I landed up in Sudan for a while.'

'And what was she doing there?'

'Volunteer work. With a famine relief programme. She's dedicated her life to that sort of work.'

He said all this with an offhand air, but I could see how seriously he took it. He intrigued me at moments like these. He seemed so simple and straightforward, and then he showed you he was not.

'And where is she now, your girlfriend?'

'Lesotho. She came down to South Africa to be closer to me, but then she got involved with this other aid organization, and then . . .' He trailed off, looking happy. 'That's just how she is.'

He was proud of her, of his relationship with her, but something about it was odd. It was almost as if he was relieved that she was far away and that all their intimacy had to be conducted ritually, through photographs and letters. They wrote regularly to each other, once a week. I looked at her handwriting on the envelopes that arrived: strong, upright, clear. It didn't resemble his spidery uncertain hand. But somehow their whole relationship consisted in this back-and-forth of envelopes, or the formal gesture of the shrine above his bed.

Not all of the photographs over the bed were of his girlfriend. One was of an older woman, dark, thin, her hair tied back. She was smile-scowling for the camera.

'Your mother?'

He shook his head quickly. 'Sister.'

'Your sister? But she looks so much . . .'

'Older? I know. There's a big gap between us. In a way she's really like my mother. She raised me when my parents were killed.'

'I didn't know that. I'm sorry.'

'Oh, that's okay. It was long ago.' He told me how his mother and father had died in a car accident twenty-five years before. 'I was a baby still, I don't remember them.' And how his sister, who was twenty then, had taken him over and brought him up. He'd lived with her in a poor neighbourhood of a depressed coastal town, the name of which I'd never heard before. The first time he'd ever left home was when he'd won a scholarship to study medicine.

He told me all these details in a light, quick voice, as if none of it was important. But I could see that it did matter very much to him.

I said, 'I lost my mother too, when I was small.'

'Really?'

'I was ten. So I do remember. She died of leukaemia.'

'That's why you became a doctor,' he said.

It was a declaration, not a question; it startled me.

'I don't think so,' I said.

'When was the moment when you knew, you really knew, that you wanted to be a doctor?'

'I don't think I had a moment like that.'

'Never?'

'No.'

'But why not?'

'I don't know,' I said. 'I just didn't.'

He smiled. 'I know when mine was. Exactly.'

He was like that. A grand design ran through everything. The moment of his realization was a story he'd told himself over and over.

'I was twelve years old. My parents were buried in the cemetery near our house and my sister always said that one day she would take me to visit them. But she never took me. So I decided to go by myself.

'I used to pass there every day, all those crosses in the ground. So this one day I just turned in at the gate and started looking. I walked and walked. It was a hot day. I'd never seen so many dead people. Just rows and rows of them. I went up and down, up and down, looking. But I couldn't find them.

'I started crying. It was too much. But then this old black guy found me. He was working there, he was wearing a uniform, a sort of white coat, he had a list of the people who were buried there. He had a map. But he couldn't find my parents.'

'Why not?'

'I don't know. I told him my father's name—Richard. But he said there wasn't a Richard Waters on the map. I just cried and cried.

'He was very kind to me. He took me to his little office, he gave me tea and bread. He talked to me for a bit. Then I felt better and I went home. My sister was there.'

'Did you tell her?'

His eyes dropped. '*Ja*. And that was the moment. I can't explain. She was also very good, hugging me and everything, telling me that one day we would go to the graves together. But it all got mixed up in me—her kindness, the old black guy . . .'

'His white coat,' I said. Two could play at this pseudo-psychology of his.

'The white coat,' he said musingly. 'Yes. You may be right about that, Frank. The idea came to me right then.'

'That you should be a doctor.'

'Yes. It wasn't clear like that, you know, but . . . the seed was there. From that moment.'

'Because of your parents.'

'That's how I knew it must be the same for you. Your mother's death. Mine was because of my parents too. I think we're very similar, Frank.'

'But I never had a moment like that,' I said.

'Maybe you don't remember it,' he said. 'But you did.'

He was very insistent about it, but I knew there'd never been a clear moment like that for me. I'd never had a burning sense of vocation—just uneasy ambition and a need to impress my father. But the question he'd put to me stayed in my mind, bothering me. I felt that I should have had a moment of truth like his. It was only long afterwards that I wondered whether his revelation from the graveyard had ever actually happened at all.

He never mentioned it again. He was too busy asking other questions. When he wanted to know something, he had no sense of delicacy or restraint. Sometimes he alarmed me, but I also found myself telling him things I'd never discussed before.

My marriage, for instance. This wasn't a subject on which I felt inclined to open up to anybody. Not that it was charged with a lot of pain any more—the nerves were dead—but it was still private and unexposed. But a week or two after he came, Laurence plunged right in.

'I notice you still wear your wedding ring.'

'That's because I'm still married.'

'Really? But where's your wife?'

And in a moment I was telling him all sorts of delicate details—how Karen had run off with Mike, my best friend from army days and one-time partner in practice. How they were living together now and how my retreat up here had somehow stalled the divorce process so that we were still technically man-and-wife.

'And when will it all be over?'

'I don't know,' I said. 'Some time in the next six months. She's got the whole divorce process moving along again lately. I think they're in a hurry to leave the country.'

'Is she getting married again?'

'I think that's the idea.'

'To this guy? Your friend from the army?'

'Mike? *Ja,* she's still with him. She says he's the great love of her life.'

'He was never your friend, Frank,' he told me solemnly. 'No true friend would ever do that to you.'

'I am aware of that, Laurence.'

'I would never do that. Never, never, never.'

'That's good.'

'I wouldn't wear that ring any more,' he said. 'Why do you wear it, Frank?'

'I don't know,' I said. 'Habit.' But the golden glint on my finger was more a symbol than a habit. I closed my hand into a fist to hide it.

When he said, 'I would never do that to you,' he was telling me that he was a true friend. I think he felt that way almost from the first day. Yet the feeling wasn't mutual. He was a room-mate to me, a temporary presence who was disturbing my life.

But I found myself spending a lot of time with Laurence. In some respects I didn't have a choice: in the room, at work, he'd been assigned to me. Yet outside of that, and almost imperceptibly, we started to keep each other company. It became something of a ritual, for instance, to play table tennis in the recreation room. I'd never spent much time there before; it was a sad room. But somehow it was not unpleasant to bat the plastic ball back and forth across the table, talking in a desultory way. Most of our conversations were like that: weightless, aimless, passing the time.

And we went on a few walks together. It had been years since I'd gone off on those long hikes of mine; now we started again. I don't remember who first suggested it, him or me, but he'd got hold of a large map from somewhere of the surrounding countryside. Most of the time he kept it stuck to the wall above his bed, but once a week at least he took it down and planned routes for us to try on our days off. We packed sandwiches and beer and set off on various trails through the bush. I took him on some of the old walks, too, that I remembered, some of them with spectacular views. These outings were mostly happy and relaxed, though he was never quite at home out there, in the wild.

We also went down, more and more often, to Mama Mthembu's place in the evenings. This wasn't new to me, of course; I had been there many times before. But it had been my habit to drop by in the late afternoon occasionally; I didn't enjoy the crowded and smoky atmosphere that took over at night. All the off-duty staff from the hospital were usually there, and the enforced intimacy over glasses of alcohol could be oppressive. But now, with Laurence in tow, it felt somehow more inviting.

At Mama's place, after-hours, none of the divisions and hierarchy of the work situation applied. Themba and Julius, the two kitchen workers, were on a level with Jorge and Claudia. Sometimes Dr Ngema even joined these gatherings as an uneasy equal. And though I never relaxed completely, some of Laurence's equanimity in these situations transferred itself to me, so that I became less distant and aloof.

One morning, after one of these late-night sessions, I found myself alone with Jorge at the breakfast table. He sucked benignly on his moustache and said, 'The young man. Your friend. He is a good young man.'

'Who? Laurence? He isn't my friend.'

'No? But you are everywhere together.'

'Dr Ngema put us in the same room. But I don't know him well.'

'He is a good young man.'

'I'm sure he is. But he's not my friend yet.'

It was strange, but I felt uncomfortable at being linked with Laurence in this way. The word 'friend' had associations for me. Mike had been my friend, until he ran off with my wife. Since then I hadn't made any friends. I didn't want anyone getting too close to me.

But the word kept coming up. Your friend did this. Your friend was there. How is your friend? And every time I heard it, the term became a little more worn with use, so that it didn't have that sharp edge any more.

'Did you have your talk with our new friend?' Dr Ngema asked me one day, as we walked back to the residential block together.

'What talk?'

It was an indication, perhaps, of how much had changed that I had no idea what she meant.

'You know. You were going to show him around . . . discuss the possibility of transferring him somewhere else.'

'Oh, yes. Yes, I did. But he's happy here. He doesn't want to go.'

'Well, that's a first,' she said. Our feet crunched companionably through the gravel together. 'Maybe,' she said after a while, 'you could pressure him a bit.'

'Actually, I don't mind having him around.'

'Yes? So can I take it that you're happy to share your room?'

This was a different question, separate to what had gone before.

'No,' I said. 'Ruth, if anything comes up . . . The Santanders' room, any other room, I'd appreciate it.'

'I'll bear it in mind,' she told me.

But I knew from that moment that nothing was going to change: Laurence would stay in my room.

'They're not going,' he announced one day, while we sat on duty together.

'Who?'

'The Santanders. You told me they were leaving and I was moving to their room. But I was talking to them yesterday and they said they're staying here.'

As it happened, I had overheard part of the same conversation, so I knew that he didn't have the whole picture. I was sitting at the table when he was in the recreation room with them, locked in earnest debate, and I hung back to listen.

'But why South Africa?' Laurence was saying.

'Opportunity,' Jorge said.

'Exactly. Opportunity. The chance to make a difference. There can't be a lot of places in the world where that's possible right now.'

'Yes, yes,' Jorge intoned solemnly.

'Better money,' Claudia said. 'Good house.'

'Yes, well, that too. But I'm talking about something different.'

'You are talking about what?'

'I believe it's only the beginning. Of this country. The old history doesn't count. It's all starting now. From the bottom up. So I want to be here. I don't want to be anywhere else in the world, where it doesn't matter if I'm there or not. It matters that I'm here.'

The Santanders were a middle-aged couple from Havana. They'd been sent out a couple of years before as part of a large group of doctors imported by the Health Department to help with the staffing crisis. He was a plump, affable man with a big moustache and a genial intelligence. His wife was slightly hysterical, a good-looking older woman with not much English. My brief affair with Claudia a year before had left her permanently embittered towards me. They had the room next door to mine and there had been many nights, more and more of them lately, when their voices carried in strident

Spanish argument through the wall. It was an open secret that she wanted to go home, she didn't want to stay, while he wanted to make a future here. Their marriage was cracked down the middle.

'This country depends,' Laurence said fervently, 'on people like you. Committed people, who want to make a difference.'

'Yes, yes,' Jorge said.

'They tell us, good house, good car,' Claudia said. 'But they don't tell us, Soweto. Ooh, Soweto!' I could picture her shudder.

'I wouldn't mind being in Soweto,' Laurence said. 'But this is better. This is really nowhere.'

I knew a little bit about how the Santanders felt towards Soweto. Claudia had told me during the throes of our affair. It was their first posting in the country, the place they wanted to go to. Maybe, like Laurence, they wanted to make a difference. But they couldn't handle the cases that came in all the time. The violence, the extremity of it, was something they'd never seen. On Saturday nights in the emergency room it was knife-wounds and shotgun blasts and maimings and gougings with broken bottles. 'Like war,' Claudia wailed, 'like big war outside all the time!' And this was on top of the usual load of illnesses and accidents that the hospital could barely deal with. After six months or so they asked for a transfer and landed up here.

In a certain sense it was her time in Soweto that led to my affair with Claudia. In the first few weeks after she'd arrived here a woman was rushed in one night. She'd been attacked by a lynch mob in her village that had stabbed and beaten her and tried to burn her to death for being a witch. Her condition was critical. It was clear that she would die, but we all ran around madly, trying to do what we could. In the end she did die. An ambulance came from the nearest hospital to take the body away and then afterwards, in the empty anticlimax of the small hours of the night, Claudia and I were left alone in the office. And suddenly her neutral mask cracked and fell. She started to cry and shake uncontrollably and what was present in the room was all the pent-up months of horror at what she'd seen in this country for the first time in her life. 'How can people do like this?' she cried, 'how, how?'

I put my arms around her to comfort her, while she sobbed like a little child. I knew, I could feel, where this was coming from. Something in this country had gone too far, something had snapped. It was like a fury so strong that it had come loose from its moorings. I could only hold her to console her, but then consolation turned to something else. It was very powerful—lust fuelled by grief. We were like animals that first night. But it went on for weeks, meeting each other in deserted wards or the corners of dark passages. It was in the long empty time after I'd stopped seeing Maria, and it filled up a lack for me. I had nothing to lose. But she had a lot to lose, and the danger of what we were doing was crazy. We could be caught at any time. At least we never met in my room, because it was only one wall away from her husband.

But I think he knew. Since that time there had always been an uneasy tension between us, which may of course have been merely my guilt. It was only lately, now that Laurence was around, that some of this tension had eased.

'But they are leaving,' I told him now. 'That's definite. It's just a matter of when.'

'I don't think so. They're a lovely, committed couple.'

'Committed to what?'

'Well, you know. The country. The future. All that.'

'Come on,' I said. 'They don't tell anyone, but it's an open secret. Everyone knows it.'

'Jorge told me Cuba is a hole.'

'Ja, all right,' I said. 'It's complicated. Jorge doesn't want to go back, but she does. They fight about it all the time.'

'You assume that she'll win.'

'She will win.'

'Bullshit,' he said. 'Anyway, they don't fight.'

'Haven't you heard them through the wall?'

'No. Definitely not.'

'Anyway,' I said irritably, 'it's not the Santanders' room you'll be moving to. It's Tehogo's room.'

'Tehogo's room?'

I don't know where this came from. I just suddenly said it, but the minute the words were out they took on the vehemence of truth.

'Yes,' I said. 'Tehogo's room. He's not supposed to be there in any case. He'll be moving out soon.'

'Where's he going to?'

'I don't know,' I said. 'It doesn't matter.'

Tehogo's room—the last one in our corridor, on the left—was meant to be occupied by a doctor. But Tehogo wasn't a doctor. He was a nurse. Strictly speaking, in terms of qualifications, he wasn't even that. But he did the work at the hospital that a nurse was supposed to do.

He had been here longer than me. When I arrived he was already installed in the room. How he had come to be there was never fully explained to me, but it was all tied up with troubles in the homeland from years before. What was certain was that his family—mother and father, brother and uncle—had been killed in one or another act of political violence. It seemed there was some kind of tie by marriage to the Brigadier himself, and the killings were meant as revenge.

All that was murky. The only clear element to emerge was Tehogo himself, orphaned and alone, with nowhere to go. At that time he was working at the hospital as an enrolled nurse, but he kept failing his exams; he was kept on for want of any other candidates. He'd been living out, staying with his family and coming in each day to work. It was only because he was at the hospital that he'd escaped being murdered himself. But now he couldn't go back to his home.

Dr Ngema gave him the room. It seems it was meant as an interim measure, just until he found his feet again. But he had stayed.

The other nursing staff had gone and he'd gradually taken over their work, till now he was the only person left who could or would do the countless little petty labours involved—being a porter, washing and feeding patients, cleaning floors, taking messages. He was, if not on duty, at least on permanent call, so it made sense for him to be living there, in the grounds. But there may have been more to it than that. This part was also hearsay and rumour, but there was a story that the Brigadier had made a personal appeal to Dr Ngema to allow his young relative to stay.

This was told to me by the other white doctor who'd worked here until a few years ago. He was bitter and burnt-out, and I didn't attach too much importance to his gossip. But it was obvious that Dr Ngema had an interest in Tehogo that went deeper than the professional side of things. She was solicitous and concerned. At staff meetings she went out of her way to draw him into discussions, she called him into her office for personal chats, and once she'd asked me if I would keep an eye on him.

I tried to do what she asked. But it was hard to get near to Tehogo. He was sullen and sour, continually drawn in on some dark core in himself. He seemed to have no friends, except for one young man from outside the hospital who was frequently hanging around. I tried not to blame him; of course he must be embattled with the terrible loss of his family. But the truth was that he didn't look like much of a victim. He was young and good-looking, and he was always dressed in natty new clothes. He had an earring in one ear and a silver chain around his neck. There was money coming to him from somewhere, but this was never mentioned by anybody. We had to treat him as poor Tehogo, dispossessed and damaged, and it was curious how powerful his powerlessness could be. He wouldn't talk, except in grudging syllables, and even those were always given in reply to something he'd been asked. He never showed any interest in my life, and so it was difficult to be interested in his. For a long time now he had been a silent presence at the dark end of the passage, or sitting at the edge of staff meetings, saying nothing. I hardly noticed him.

But now Laurence Waters had come, and I had to notice Tehogo. I noticed him because he was in the doctor's room where Laurence should be. But what I'd said to Laurence was untrue: Tehogo wasn't moving anywhere. There was no space and nowhere for him to go.

'Oh. Well,' Laurence said. 'He's a strange person, Tehogo. I try to talk to him, but he's very . . .'

'I know what you mean.'

After a pause he said forlornly, 'I like sharing with you, Frank.'

'Do you?' I felt bad now, for my irritation as well as the lie. 'Maybe it won't happen.'

'Do you think so?'

'It's possible,' I said. 'It's possible we'll all just stay where we are.'

6

Laurence couldn't sit still in one place for very long. He had a restless, angular energy that burned him up. If he wasn't pacing and smoking, he was stalking around the grounds, looking at things, asking questions. Why are the walls painted pink? Why is the food so bad? Why hasn't all this wasted space been used? Why, why, why—there was something childlike about it. But he also had an adult resourcefulness that wanted things to be different.

One afternoon I came back to the room to find him struggling with the door at the end of the passage.

'What are you doing?'

'Come and give me a hand.'

He was trying to put a chain and padlock around the handle of the door. There was no bolt in the wall, so he had to loop one end around a metal bracket for a fire extinguisher, which had either been stolen or had never been supplied.

'It would be much easier just to get a key for the door,' I told him.

'There isn't one. I've been looking. Dr Ngema let me search through all the spares.'

'What do you want to lock it for anyway?'

He blinked in surprise. 'You should know. You saw what's going on in there.'

I had to think about it before I realized that he was talking about all the stripping and stealing that had taken place in the deserted wing.

'But that's old. And what difference does it make anyway?'

'What difference?' He smiled uncertainly. 'Are you being serious? It shouldn't happen.'

'Laurence, Laurence.'

'What?'

I helped him fasten the chain around the wall bracket and lock it. But you could see at a glance that the padlock was cheap and weak. You could break it with a blow.

That was the sort of thing he did. On one of the days that followed I found him cutting the grass in the open plot between our bedroom and the main wing. In all the years I'd been there nobody had ever touched that grass. There was no mower, so he'd got hold of an old rusty scythe from somewhere. He was red in the face and sweating, and the work was slow. On the back step of the recreation room, Themba and Julius, the kitchen staff, were watching him with baffled amusement.

'Your friend is crazy,' Julius said to me.

'Well, it'll look better afterwards,' I said.

I supposed that was the point. And when the brown heaps of dense, dead grass had been carried off behind the kitchen to the new compost heap that Laurence had started there, the ground between the two buildings was bare and clean. It did look good.

But Laurence only frowned at it and stood, panting.

'What's the matter? That's a big job you did.'

'Yes. I know.'

'Aren't you satisfied with yourself?'

'Yes, I am,' he said. 'I am.'

But he didn't look satisfied to me.

And the next day he was up on the roof, pulling out the weeds and grass that were growing there. The sun was hot and in the middle of the day his tall figure waxed and waned in laborious isolation. I took him a bottle of water and stood up there with him while he drank it.

'Nobody's going to thank you for this,' I said.

'Thank me? How do you mean?'

'I don't understand why you're bothering.'

'The roof should be clean.'

'Maybe. But it makes no difference. And the stuff will only grow back.'

'It doesn't matter,' he said stubbornly. 'It looks better when it's done.' And the roof did look clean afterwards, like the ground he'd cleared down below. From where we were standing we had a view out over the town and the rolling hills near by, and the high expansiveness made me feel satisfied and complete, as if I too had been working the whole day.

But of course I was right: the weeds and the grass did grow back, and as the slow green millimetres accumulated nobody said a word. And nobody cut them down. Laurence's attention had moved on to a new project somewhere else. And when I saw, a month or two later, that somebody had broken the cheap lock on the chain that held the door at the end of the passage, I said nothing about that either.

I had my own preoccupations. Not all of my life was centred on Laurence or the hospital: I had other pursuits, further afield, to distract me. I had gone back to visiting Maria at night. Not every night, not in the same way as before. But once or twice a week a restless impulse came over me and I headed for my car.

The sex was different now. Something hard and brutal and hungry had come into it. Maybe it was only sex now—the romance of it had gone. I was rough with her. Not violent, but with an inclination towards it that threw everything off balance. I was always on top, I held her down. And there was an answering passivity, an acquiescence, in her. But we didn't really touch each other. We didn't even try to talk. It was as if I was looking for something I couldn't get to; the closest I could come was by hammering, hammering, on this heavy wooden door.

I paid her every time now. And that's what it was: a payment. Our meetings were transactions, the limits of which were practical. When we did talk it was about arrangements. A couple of times she warned me not to come on particular nights. I accepted these restrictions without letting them conjure any personal feelings. The other man didn't exist, except as a prohibition on my time, or as a symbol in the form of a white car outside the shack.

Only once did the distance close up; she said, 'Where is that man—your friend?'

I took a moment to understand. 'Laurence? He's not my friend.'

'No?'

'No. Well, maybe he is.' I watched her pulling her dress over her head, slipping her arms into the broken sleeves. 'Why do you want to know about him?'

She gestured.

'His face . . . ?'

'Yes.'

'What about his face?'

She was about to answer, but then shook her head. A glance went between us and then it was back: the enormous distance, the wall. 'You come Friday?' she said.

So he was here too, a manic disconcerting figure, flickering for an instant on the wooden side of the shack. It was hard to imagine that my life had been entirely free of Laurence Waters just two months before.

I didn't tell him about Maria, I don't know why. Everything had been set in that first alarming instant when he asked me, 'Have you slept with that woman?' My answer was instantaneous and a lie; there was no strategy behind it. My instinct saw his intuition as a threat; I lied to defend myself. And then I had to go on lying.

I lied even though he knew exactly where I was going. The fact that he never asked made it clear that he knew. He watched me shower and change my clothes and drive off into the dark without saying anything to me. Sometimes he was still awake when I got back. The others in the hospital had seen my late comings and goings for a long time too, and none of them said anything either. But they could only guess; he knew.

So that even this little part of my life—paid for with cash, to keep it separate from the rest—became connected to Laurence.

As the weeks went past and we became more accustomed—or resigned—to each other, my mind kept going back to that question he'd asked when he first arrived. *When was the moment when you knew that you wanted to be a doctor?* I watched Laurence when he attended to the one or two patients who drifted through. It didn't matter how old or young they were, how arbitrary or critical their condition; he was the same with every one of them: serious, concerned, committed. They all seemed to matter to him.

This bothered me. It bothered me because, really, I didn't care too much. I don't mean that I didn't try. I gave my detached, professional best to each of them, but when nothing more was possible I didn't think about it again. And Laurence's involvement and effort showed up a lack in me.

I searched through my life for a moment of truth like his. It felt to me that somewhere, some time, something had happened to define me. But I couldn't bring that moment to mind.

And then I could. One arbitrary day it came to me: a simple flash of recognition. And I wished I could forget about it again.

My moment had come thirteen years before. I had spoken with Laurence, on a few occasions, in a casual, everyday way, about my time in the army. He'd asked me some questions too, with a young man's ingenuous curiosity. But every time the topic came up I could hear that it didn't mean anything real to him. It was the way he said the word 'army'. I could hear that he had no idea of what it was, what it was like. Conscription had been part of the life of every white man for forty years and then suddenly, overnight, a new law was passed and it vanished. Now here was this white man, one generation away from me, who looked on this part of my life as history.

On one or other day it happened that Laurence and I were driving yet another untreatable patient to the other hospital. The side road that linked the town to the main road was a winding one, going over hills and through dips, and from a particular turn along the way it was possible to see the remains of the military camp from which the Brigadier had come. In the old days, apparently, it used to be a major military settlement: rows and rows of tents and trucks, swarms of men moving around. That was in the time of upheaval, with the possibility of incursions from over the border. Now it was abandoned—a huddle of tatty tents behind a scrawl of barbed wire. A dirt track led off to it, but the track was overgrown and I'd never gone down there to investigate. But I always slowed down, at this particular point, to look. I don't know what the attraction was; there was nothing, really, to see. But today I thought I glimpsed a human figure, moving between the tents. It was far away and tiny and then it flashed out of sight; and I was immediately unsure whether I'd seen anything at all. But I kept turning around to look.

'What is it?' Laurence said. 'What's the matter?'

'Nothing,' I said. 'It's gone.'

I didn't want to talk about the Brigadier again to someone who didn't care who he was.

'What's that place?'

'Old army camp.'

He said, 'I wish I'd been in the army. It feels like I missed out on a formative experience.'

'You don't know what you're talking about.'

He looked sharply at me, a startled sidelong glance. 'I thought you told me it wasn't a big deal. You had a boring time, you said.'

'It was boring.'

'But?'

'I don't want to talk about this.'

He let it go, but somehow this conversation had stirred something up for me. That night I lay awake for a long time, thinking. My experience in the military didn't often come to mind; it was more like a blankness, a dead patch in my memory. There was really only one incident, one telling little encounter, that had burned itself into me.

History had sent me up to the Angolan border for two years. What I'd said to Laurence was true: most of those months were flat and dull—lost time. I got moved around from camp to camp. I had just qualified as a doctor, so I was given the rank of lieutenant. But there were quite a few of us and I did nothing to distinguish myself in any way. It seemed a good policy to lie low.

At only one point in that whole period did I ever come close to physical action. That was when I was sent for three months to a small camp deep in the bush. My experience in the military till then had been tame and domestic. I dealt with people who'd injured themselves in accidents or were suffering from heat-stroke or tick-bite fever or broken bones. Mundane calamities. But up there the casualties were of a different kind. That camp was being used for a lot of intensive activity: patrols were going out constantly, looking for enemy patrols to annihilate. For the first time I was treating people who were fighting in a war. I saw things there I hadn't seen before. Wounds made by grenades and bullets and land mines; the deliberate damage that people wilfully inflict on each other. The overriding impression that I retain is of the vividness of bleeding meat, like some kind of bright fruit blooming against the dun, dusty veld.

There were only two lieutenants in the little field hospital—me and Mike. That was where I met and befriended the man who would later run off with my wife. But in those days he was just good company. We worked under a fat captain, who was the chief medic. The officer in charge of the whole camp was Commandant Moller.

Until this one particular night, I had never come close enough to see him properly. It was his figure I saw, usually off in the distance, getting into or out of helicopters, inspecting things, giving orders. He was thin and compact and powerful and he exuded a quality of danger. We were afraid of him and went out of our way to avoid him. He had a reputation that spread far beyond his physical presence—for a blind and holy devotion to his job.

His job was killing enemy soldiers, and it was for this reason only that the camp existed. It was for this reason only that we were there, although we didn't kill anybody. No, we patched up the people who did the killing, so that they could go out and do it again. When we failed, our patients were sent out in the other direction, south, in body-bags.

I didn't have moral qualms about my job. The truth is that I didn't think about it much. I was too young, maybe, too narrow in my understanding; I saw in front of me only the immediate task at hand. Close up this wound. Pick out shrapnel. Save the life. I was a doctor, and I performed within the scope of my training. If a wounded enemy soldier had been set down in front of me, I would've reacted with the same tiny, myopic, amoral focus.

Except for that one night.

It happened from time to time that our boss, the captain, was called away at odd hours to the cell block at the centre of the camp. These summonses came after batches of Swapo prisoners were brought in, and we understood that the call had something to do with them. We understood also that we shouldn't ask too much about it. There was a lot of activity around those low brick buildings—the only permanent structures in the whole place— that was obscured by a fog of secrecy and silence. When he came back, the captain—usually a jolly, benevolent man—always seemed troubled and quiet.

But on one particular night the call came when the captain wasn't there. I forget what happened exactly, but he was away in a different camp somewhere. It was only me and Mike, sharing a bottle of whisky and talking about our plans to set up a practice together when these two years were over.

The corporal who'd brought the summons went away again. But ten minutes later he was back.

'The commandant says one of you must come.'

We looked at each other. Neither of us wanted to go.

'You do it.'

'No, you.'

'Your Afrikaans is better.'

Two minutes later I was following the brown back of the corporal through the hot dark towards the cells. I was afraid of the commandant and what he could do to me; this fear eclipsed the undefined reason I was being brought here, which might hurt me far more deeply.

The brown back led me to a tiny room with brick walls and a concrete floor. No windows. A low zinc roof, from which one raw light bulb is suspended on a length of flex. There are four soldiers here, two of them are officers. One is Commandant Moller. He is wearing his brown army pants and boots and a white T-shirt. He sits on a stool, relaxed and informal.

On the floor is a black man, naked. He is splattered with blood and lying still, except for the painful rise and fall of his ribcage as he breathes. At the periphery of my vision I see quirts and other objects, strange shapes that I don't recognize. But I know the scene, although I have never been in it before; it's an old tableau, in which my place is immediately clear.

'Naand, Lieutenant,' the commandant says. 'Jammer om te steur.'

This is the closest I have come to him. For the first time I raise my head and look into his eyes. His gaze is blue and dead. He is not unattractive, with the cold, symmetrical face of a religious idol, his brown hair cut close to the neat planes of his skull. And yet the most obvious feature of his face is not its cleanness. Military regulations stipulate that you shave in a line between ear and edge of nose, and he'd followed the rule to the letter: high on each cheekbone is a small clump of hair.

What kind of a man is this?

He says, *Is jy Engels of Afrikaans?'*

'English, Commandant.'

He switches to accentless English, his tone level and amiable. 'We need a bit of help from you, Lieutenant. You are a doctor, *né*?'

'Yes, Commandant.'

'We are busy with a little interrogation here. But our friend is taking some strain. He says he can't breathe properly. Could you just take a look at him?'

I go to the body on the floor. Even a glance can tell you that he is badly hurt. There are bruises and swellings on his face and upper body and some kind of laceration on his neck. His breathing is very audible, a high thin wheezing.

'Commandant,' I say. 'He doesn't look good.'

'Okay,' the level voice says behind me. 'But is he faking it?'

'Faking?' The question is absurd. The man needs a hospital bed, stitches, disinfectant, care. 'I don't understand.'

In a patient tone, the commandant says, 'His breathing, Lieutenant. Is there a problem?'

It's difficult to isolate his breath from the other abrasions and afflictions, but when I do I can hear the problem immediately. 'He's having an asthma attack, Commandant. He's not faking it.'

'Can you do something for him?'

'I can try. I need some water.'

'Gee vir bom water daar.'

Somebody brings me a bucket half-filled with water, in which a bloody foam is floating. I am moving now in darkness, watching myself through a long tunnel as I splash water on to his face, wipe at his wounds, to clear away the dirt and blood. This will do nothing for his asthma, but it's my instinct to try to clean him up. He stirs and groans, but the sound from his lungs goes on and on. So I open my bag of supplies and take out the nebulizer.

After a minute or two his breathing is easier.

'*Daarsy,*' one of the others says.

'*Uitstekend,*' the commandant says. 'Now I need to ask you some-thing, Lieutenant. In your opinion, as a doctor, how much more can he take?'

I stand up and turn around, but I dare not meet his eyes. I am shivering in the warm air. 'Commandant,' I say, 'he needs medical care.'

'That's not what I asked you.' The tone has hardened now. 'I'm asking you: can he take more questioning?'

'Not too much.'

'How much?'

'Commandant, if you let me give him some proper care, I can get rid of the asthma completely. He should be on cortisone.'

Somebody, one of the onlookers, says, 'Proper care,' and laughs.

'Is he about to die, Lieutenant?'

'It depends. If he gets pushed too far . . .'

'So if we go carefully . . .?'

These questions are insane, they are the measuring-points of an inverted world, doctors are here to heal and repair, not assist in this calculated demolition of nerves and flesh. I open my mouth to speak but I can feel the dead eyes of the commandant staring at me, staring me down.

There is a pause, in which I remember who I am, where I am, what is required of me. The man on the floor is an enemy, who will in any case not last the night. It is myself I must look after, so that I don't find myself in his place, naked on my back in a cell, not a doctor any more, a patient for whom there will never be a cure.

'No,' I say. 'He won't die yet.'

'Thank you, Lieutenant.' The amiable tone is back again. 'Give my regards to the captain when he gets back.'

And then I am trotting through the dark again, away from the cell and the moment of truth that has come to lodge at the dead centre of my life.

Mike was waiting for me when I got back. 'What did he want? Why did he call you?'

'*Ag*, it was nothing,' I said. 'He had a headache.'

My agony lasted only a few days. By the next morning I was already learning to bury it:

It would have made no difference.

You didn't have a choice.

You only answered the question.

And by the time I was transferred, to a dull camp where nothing of much consequence was going on, I had accepted my failure as an inevitable part of my position. I hardly thought about it again, except at odd moments when it surfaced with a strange, anomalous power.

Like now. It was as if somebody had pushed a finger through a weak place in the fabric of my past and was looking in through the hole. And I had the odd temptation to look in too and see myself from outside. But I couldn't do it. I had found my grand defining moment, but what it revealed I didn't want to know.

7

I came back from visiting Maria one night to find him sitting on his bed with his map spread out in front of him. It was very late and the whole hospital, except for the front office, was dark. But Laurence was wide awake.

'What are you doing?'

'Planning. What are you doing tomorrow?'

'Tomorrow is my day off.'

'So do you want to come on an outing with me?'

'To where?'

'Just a little walk. It's a surprise. Come on, Frank.'

'All right,' I said. 'Why not?'

I thought of this as one more of the little hikes we'd been on together. But it wasn't the same. Right from the start there was a sense of a mission about him. I woke twice in the night and he was still sitting there on his bed, gazing at the map. And he woke me at eight-thirty, tense with excitement. He had a rucksack packed full of things—sandwiches and beer and suntan lotion.

It was a clean, clear morning, the grass shining like metal. We drove towards the border. In the villages we passed people were drawing water, washing themselves, preparing food on fires. The big landscape was stirring with early life. Trees and plants seemed to strain powerfully upwards, throwing themselves vertically against the force of gravity. On either side there were dirt tracks leading off, some signposted to farms or little settlements, others nameless. We took one of the unmarked ones to the left. His car lurched and toiled between the ruts, but today even this felt like part of the life and vibration of the land. After a little way the track started to follow the dark line of a river. And then it petered out in an overgrown spot, cool with shadow. Past a screen of bamboo I could see the water flowing. It was small, more like a stream than anything, but the trees around it drew up a rich green life.

He stood peering into the water. 'I bet there are fish in here,' he said. 'Do you fish, Frank?'

'I used to. But it got boring.'

'I bet you need patience to fish. Do you think there are crocodiles?'

'Too small for that.'

He looked relieved. It was obvious that he was more uneasy than usual out here, in the wild. We set out, up the river, trudging through mud and splashing through the water. I let him go ahead, the overloaded rucksack labouring through thickets, now and then his anxious face turning back to blink at me. From time to time he stopped to consult the map, though we kept to the water all the way. I felt happy—happier than I'd been in months. I'd forgotten how good it was to be away from buildings and people and familiar objects. It was cool and lovely under the trees.

In places we had to clamber on rocks and in other places we had to wade. I didn't mind floundering through the dark water, but his face was lopsided with alarm. 'Are you sure there aren't any crocodiles?' he said again. 'Not sure,' I said, 'but probably not.' Of course there were no crocodiles, but I enjoyed his discomfiture. After a while I went ahead to lead the way, hearing the sucking sound of his feet in the mud, his hands slapping at mosquitoes.

After an hour the water widened into a pool, edged on the far side by cliffs, from which a waterfall came down. It was a beautiful, primitive place. A fine steam of spray drifted over the rocks, wetting the leaves of ferns that grew out of the cracks.

But we'd disturbed something, a long saurian shape that flung itself into the water.

'I told you there were crocodiles!'

'That's not a crocodile,' I said, 'it's a monitor. Look at it go!'

The huge slithery form swam furiously along the base of the cliff and then hauled itself up into a crack and climbed. It went up a vertical surface and disappeared on to a ledge. The scaly ancient look of the lizard was disturbing; I couldn't get it out of my mind.

But I swam in the water. It was the obvious spot to stop and eat lunch; long shafts of sun came through the trees and the rocks were warm and solid. I took off my clothes and swam out to where the surface boiled and hissed. I felt something of what I used to feel after I'd first come up to the hospital and went on long hikes alone into the bush. But of course I wasn't alone now; I had Laurence here. My friend.

He sat on the side, knees up to his chin, watching. He looked disconsolate and perplexed. The chaos of the wilderness seemed to oppress him; I think he would have liked to uproot it all and plant lawn there. I swam closer and waved. 'Come on in!'

He shook his head. 'I'm okay here.'

'The water's great.'

'Do you want a beer?'

'Well, why don't we eat?' I dragged myself out and lay dripping on the rock. 'How about a sandwich?'

'Here?'

'Why not here?'

'I don't know, it's still early. I thought we could eat higher up.'

'Higher up? What are you talking about?'

'We're not there yet, Frank.'

'Not where yet?'

'This is an outing, remember.'

'*Ja?*'

He took his glasses off and rubbed them. His face, as he turned to me, had a clean, startled look to it. 'I haven't been completely truthful, I suppose.'

I waited for it.

'Well, truthful isn't the right word.'

'What is the right word?'

'I haven't explained everything. This is a hike, an outing I mean, of course.'

'But?'

'But there is somewhere I want to get to.'

'Where is that, Laurence?'

He put his glasses on and got the map and came to sit on the rock next to me. He'd taken off his shirt and his pale, hairless chest, knobbly with bones, looked artificial. In the room I was the shy, private one, always changing in the bathroom or under a towel, while he didn't care how I saw him. But out here our roles had somehow reversed.

'Here,' he said. He was pointing to something on the map, but I couldn't see what. I could make out the blue line of the river, but the rest of it was just altitudes and contours and the nameless dots of villages. 'I want to go there.'

'But where?'

'Here. Can't you see?' He was jabbing with the blunt tip of his finger.

'That just looks like a village to me.'

'What do you mean, just a village? It is a village.'

'But. But.' I peered into his face for an explanation. In all the short time I'd known him he'd never made a joke, but it felt as if this might be the first. He gazed steadily back at me. 'I don't understand,' I said.

'What?'

'Why do you want to go there?'

'Just to see it.'

I looked at the map. It was inexplicable to me. The whole terrain was peppered with the little marks of human settlement, some big enough for names, others not. But he had ringed one, just one. I stared at it and after a while the undulating contour lines resolved themselves into a sort of picture for me. I could make out the cliffs at the point where we were sitting. Up at the top and maybe two or three kilometres north, a little way west of the river, was his particular dot.

But of course it was nonsense; we hadn't come all this way 'just to see it'. He was after something he didn't want to talk about, and I'd sensed it from the beginning. It was curiosity that had brought me on this outing.

'You couldn't have chosen one more difficult to get to, could you?' There was no road, no path even, and the ground looked hilly and uneven.

'That's it, do you see it, that's the whole point!' He was very excited. The lenses of his glasses had picked up drops of water, so that he seemed suddenly to be weeping.

'No,' I said. 'Laurence, what is the point?'

'I wanted the most inaccessible one. I wanted one that wasn't easy to get to.'

For the first time he seemed slightly mad to me; maybe he saw this in my face, because he dropped his eyes and started toying with the corner of the map. He looked crestfallen.

'You don't want to do this, do you?'

'I don't understand what this is. What are we doing?'

'I told you,' he said stubbornly. 'I just want to see.'

'Why?'

'Just because.'

'No.'

'We don't have to climb the cliff,' he said. 'There's a way up. I can show you on the map.'

'No.'

'Come on.'

'My hike is over,' I said. 'I'll wait here. You go on alone.'

It was like a door slamming between us. I had never spoken to him in this way before, or if I had it was only as a joke. I wasn't joking now. A cold anger had come up in me against him. Who was he, this overheated boy, just out of his internship, with his forced friendship and his secret plans and schemes? I didn't like him any more and I wasn't going to follow him any further.

He could see it in my face. He was astounded. His eyes went very round and his mouth trembled, but he didn't cry. After he'd sat staring at his feet for a while he got up and started putting his shirt on, very deliberately, button by button. Then he said in a casual voice, 'All right.'

'What?'

'You stay here. I'll leave the food with you. I don't think I'll be too long. A couple of hours. See you later.'

He was already moving away. I wanted to say something, but what? In every sense he was leaving me behind. I looked into the trees and when I turned around again he'd disappeared.

I was defiant for a while. I took out the sandwiches and drank a beer. But my little moment was fading already and I was sorry for what I'd done. How bad could it be, getting to the top of the cliffs? And he'd only meant well. I had an impulse to pack up and follow him, but I didn't even know which direction he'd gone in.

Now a shadow had come over the day. And down here in the little hollow the sun had gone too. The pool was a dark mirror, its surface cracked and broken by the force of the water. The spray was cold and the outline of the cliffs crept steadily over the forest. High up there it was a hot day, but I felt chilly and alone. I remembered the monstrous lizard shape struggling in the water.

Now I felt watched. The trees were a dark cryptic presence all around me, the rocks bulged with hard inner life. It had been years since the world observed me like this; it made me a child again. I had a memory of the bottom of our garden and how huge and complex it was on the day that my mother had died.

When I set out walking it wasn't to follow him. I was still naked; I was just walking into the trees. I don't know what I was looking for. Just to move, to move. The leaves were densely packed, but there was an opening that might've been a path. An animal track down to the water. Quite quickly, the river was only a noise behind me, fading away. The dank bush thinned out into undergrowth and air, still edged with a filigree of branches, through which I was trying to find a way.

And then it was there. The house. Or rather—my first sight of it—a diamond-shaped grid of wire, overgrown with creeper and half rusted away. A fence. And beyond it, sinking into the leaves, a glimpse of a gable and a broken front door.

A house. Here. Why? I took a full step back, not to touch.

But nobody lived here. You could see that right away. Nobody had lived here for a long time. There was no trace of a garden; it was all wild and rank. The windows were glassless and black. And the fence—which was once formidable—was folding and falling in on itself.

I went over. There was a place a little way along where the fence was completely flat and you could step in. Now there was the ghost of what had long ago been a path. A few smooth stones, the faintest trace of a verge. But the flowerbeds had erased themselves, leaking and overflowing in a mess of weeds and leaves until no shape was left. I went up the front steps on to the porch. Cracks and cobwebs and watermarks. The front door was burst on its hinges. I stepped through. Why did I want to go in? *Just to see it.*

I went down a long passage with doors leading off into empty rooms, no furniture, no pictures, no objects. The place had been cleaned out, and maybe not by the owners. Other people had been here since: there were the remains of a fire, not too recent, in the corner of one room. And a scattering of cigarette butts that had paled with time. Down the long wall of the passage somebody had scratched a huge word, BEASTIE, in big drawling letters that collapsed towards each other. But in the little dunes of sand that had collected on the floor, the only footprints were mine.

It was hard to know what the rooms had been for. In one of them, the last, a cracked sink and linoleum floor gave some clue. But the others were vacant shells, with all the life hollowed out of them. In places, weeds were pushing up through the boards and in the plaster cracks were spreading like veins. From outside, the presence of the trees leaned inward on the house.

And I was afraid here. Not in the same way that the pool at the waterfall made me afraid. No, that was aloneness, and this was something else: the very opposite of being alone. There was nobody with me, but it felt as if somebody was there, just at the edge of my sight, moving around the corners before I got there. It was a faceless figure, on the verge of being human, not a personality so much as a force. Malevolent but amused. Something that this country had thrown up between me and it, conjured out of ruin and wilderness and not belonging completely to either, a shape, an outline, a threat. It meant me harm.

I left by the back door. I couldn't bring myself to walk through the house again, and it was a relief to be outside, under the sky. There was another gate at the back and a dirt road that was disappearing under grass. There was nothing to explain the house, the road, out here, or why they weren't a house and a road any more.

When I got back to the pool he was waiting.

'Where were you?'

'Over there,' I said.

'Doing what?'

'Just walking.' After a moment I added: 'There's a house in there.'

'A house? Whose house?'

'Nobody's. It's abandoned. I don't know.'

'Let's go and look.'

'No,' I said, and something in the way the word came out made his face fall. I felt suddenly self-conscious and turned away to dress as I went on: 'I think it was probably owned by a white family. They abandoned it when the area was made a homeland.'

'Really?'

'Well, I don't know that. It's a guess.'

'Maybe I'll go and have a look,' he said, but his tone was half-hearted.

'How was your village?'

'I didn't get there.' He cast a frustrated glance up the cliff.

'What happened?'

'I don't know, the map . . . Something was wrong. Maybe it isn't there any more.' There were thorns and blackjacks stuck to his clothes and he was pent-up, hands knotting and unknotting at his sides. He waited until I was fully dressed. 'Frank, I'm sorry about earlier.'

'It's all right.'

'No, I should've told you. It wasn't fair to spring it on you like that. But I thought you might enjoy the excursion.'

'I have enjoyed it.'

'Really?'

'Really.' The dark feeling was lifting and it was pleasant to be out here again. But something was still unexpressed and the weight of it made us silent as we went back down the river.

We might never have talked about it at all. But late that night we were woken up by a crash against the wall, then volleys of screaming in Spanish. The Santanders were having a terrible argument next door. There was no hint as to what might've started it, especially as one of them was meant to be on duty in the office at the time.

Laurence shot up out of bed in a panic. His white underpants and T-shirt hovered uneasily in the middle of the floor.

'Jesus Christ,' he said. 'What is that?'

'The lovely committed couple. They're murdering each other.'

'What do you mean? Are they having a fight?'

I said, 'I told you.'

He listened to them. 'Jesus Christ.'

There was another bang on the wall. It was strange, but the schism in the Santanders' marriage, across which they were always pulling and screaming at each other, was also between Laurence and me now, in the room. I got out of bed and went into the passage to knock on their door. They didn't open, but the shouting stopped immediately. Then there was a dim sound of crying that eventually tapered away.

When I got back to the room he was lying on his back on the floor, staring at the ceiling and smoking a cigarette. A sort of midnight melancholy had come over him, because he wasn't keen on the Santanders any more. 'You know, Frank,' he said sadly, 'I think you're the only one here who really understands me.'

'Come on.'

'No, really. The rest—they're selfish. They don't get it.'

'I'm selfish, Laurence.'

'That's just a game with you.'

'No, it's not. I'm the most selfish person in this place, I promise you.'

'That's not true. You like to think badly about yourself, Frank. You mustn't undervalue yourself.'

'Come on. Let's go to sleep.'

'I don't think I can sleep now. What were they doing—hitting each other?'

'Something like that.'

'You're my friend, Frank. You must remember that.'

The declaration had come out of nowhere. I got into bed and pulled up the sheets. After a minute he sat up and I could feel him looking at me.

'I had this idea, you see.'

I knew immediately, without it being said, that this was the conversation we hadn't had earlier that day, by the river. I waited, and he told me: 'I've been thinking about the hospital.'

'Yes.'

'Well, it's a failure. It obviously doesn't work.'

'Yes.'

'So I thought, if the people won't come to the hospital, then let the hospital go to them.'

He drew on his cigarette. In the pause I suddenly knew, understood, everything. But I let him speak.

'I thought . . . take a village. Not just any village. The most remote one, the one that's hardest to find. And go out there. You know, with medicine. Give out condoms, talk about Aids, do vaccinations, I don't know, do something.'

'Run a clinic'

'Yes. Basically. We can't just sit at the hospital, feeling hopeless. At least let's go and tell them where the hospital is.'

'You wanted to run a clinic this morning?'

'No, no, this was just a recce. I wanted to have a look. See what they might need. I don't know what I'm getting into. Is this a crazy idea, Frank? Tell me. I need to know.'

'Yes.'

'Is it?'

'It's a fucking crazy idea, Laurence.'

'But why?'

I didn't answer him; I didn't have the words. Instead I asked, 'What is the point of finding some remote village in the middle of nowhere? You could've taken any village. The one behind Maria's place—why not?'

'Maria?' He blinked in confusion, then remembered. 'Oh, her, yes, yes.'

'So why?'

'It was just a gesture, Frank, you know? A symbol. If you can do it in the furthest place, you can do it: in the nearest one too.'

He'd done the same thing by coming to the hospital. It wasn't enough for him to go where life or fate assigned him. No, he had to grandstand with some big display that meant nothing to anybody except him. Irritably, I told him, 'Symbols have got nothing to do with medicine.'

'Haven't they?'

'Where do you come from, Laurence? What country are you living in?'

He sat in injured silence for a while, looking at his cigarette. The curtains billowed on a cool gust of wind. 'Anyway,' he said at last.

'Anyway.'

'It was only an idea. And we don't have to fight about it, because I couldn't find the village in any case.'

'I want to sleep now, Laurence. Come on. Enough.'

'Okay,' he said. He got quickly into bed. There was a long silence, full of sighing and breathing, then he said, 'Sorry, Frank.'

'It's all right.'

'I don't want to upset you.'

'It's all right.'

'Because you're my friend, Frank. I wouldn't want anything to change between us.'

'Nothing will change.'

'Do you promise that, Frank?'

'I promise that, Laurence. Good night.'

'Good night, Frank. Good night.'

8

Nothing changed. That was the way of things up there. One day resembled another in the sameness of its intentions, the level graph of its ambitions; and I'd become used to it. I wanted to keep everything fixed and rooted in its place, for ever.

Not even the seasons changed much. We were too near the tropics for that. There was a dry season and a rainy season, but the temperature that ran through them both didn't rise or fall too much on the chart.

When Laurence arrived we were in the middle of summer, the rainy season: in the afternoons there was a restless, electric sheen to the sky and thunderclouds clotted into a solid mass. When it stormed, the lightning was spectacular. Then often it cleared and in the evenings the flying ants swarmed. In the mornings the floor was full of their transparent wings. But now we had moved into winter, with its clear, brittle light. Certain trees in the forest were bare and on some mornings a thin frost lay on the ground.

None of this was different; the same things happened every year, all in their usual place. My life looked as it normally did. But somewhere deep down, underneath, it wasn't the same.

One night when I was visiting Maria, just as we'd settled down on the blanket together, I felt my sexual desire—which was almost habit by now—give way to something else: another feeling completely, subversive because it was strange.

'What's the matter?' she said.

My hands had fallen away from her. I was looking at her in the dark.

'Let's not do this tonight,' I said. 'Let's do something different. Let's talk.'

'Talk?'

'Why don't you tell me something.'

She sat up, pulling her dress straight, staring at me.

'Tell you something what?'

'I want you to tell me everything about your life.'

'I told you this everything.'

'No, but I mean really. I mean everything. I want to know where you were born. I want to know about your mother and father. Your brothers and sisters. I want to know what you thought about when you were growing up. I want to know how you got married. About your husband. Everything.'

'I told you this!' Alarm disguised itself as indignation, as if I was accusing her of something.

I went on, as if this thought was a continuation—and for me it was: 'Maria. If you want to, we can stop this. You know that? If you want me to go and never come back, you can say that to me.'

'You want finish this?'

'No. No. But if you want to, I will do what you want.'

But she shook her head. 'I don't want this talking,' she said, and rolled over on to me. She'd heard, perhaps, a false note in my voice, and her hands moved me back into the old, true tracks of habit. And nothing was different after all.

One day, while we were playing table tennis in the recreation room, Laurence said to me, 'Listen, Frank. When you have people up here to visit, where do they stay?'

'Nobody comes to visit me.'

'Never?'

'No.'

'Oh.' The plastic ball bounced off the table and rolled.

'Who's coming to visit you, Laurence?'

'Zanele. My girlfriend. You know, from Lesotho.'

He hadn't mentioned her for months. Every week or so, the letters on fine coloured paper came and went between them, but nothing more than that. The little shrine of photographs above his bed was gathering dust. There were none of the breathless phone calls, the urgent longings, that I remembered from when I was young. I'd begun to doubt her existence.

But now she was coming up for a weekend. She hadn't been able to come before now, he told me, because of her commitments in Lesotho.

'There must be a hotel or something.'

I shook my head. 'There was Mama Mthembu's place, but she closed down that side of it. No business.'

'Maybe she'd let out a room as a favour.'

'Listen,' I said. 'I'll get out of our room if you need it.'

'No, no, that's not right. But it would be great if you asked Mrs Mthembu. She likes you.'

That night, on my way to visit Maria, I stopped in at Mama's to find out. I didn't think she would help, but an odd coincidence was at work. Standing around the bar were two or three men I'd never seen before, strangers in town. They were in civilian clothes, but their haircuts and their bearing looked military to me. And yes, Mama said, they were part of a group of soldiers who'd been sent up here, who were being billeted in her hotel. The old rooms were being cleaned out and made ready. Good for business, she said, smiling broadly.

'Soldiers? But what for?'

She leaned towards me confidingly. 'I think they are a border patrol. To keep foreigners out.'

'How many of them?'

'I'm not sure. Five, six. So far there are only three. But more are coming soon.'

And even this was part of the different feeling in the town. All the old rules bending, solid objects rolling out of place.

'So is there any chance that you will have an extra room for the weekend? There is a woman coming up who needs a place to stay.'

'Hmm. Maybe. But you must check with me on Thursday. You have a little girlfriend?'

'Not mine. She's visiting Laurence Waters. He's the young man who sometimes—'

'Yes, I know Laurence. He is my friend.'

'Oh,' I said. 'Yes.'

She had never learned my name, but Laurence was her friend. And still he sent me down to talk to her about a room, as if I had some special influence.

In two days the whole place was full of news of the soldiers. Different rumours flew around. But it seemed that they had been sent to plug up this stretch of the border, which was notoriously porous. Not just people, but all kinds of other illegal and dangerous goods were going back and forth: arms and ammunition, drugs, poached ivory. The name most consistently mentioned in connection with this traffic was that of the Brigadier, but all of it was gossip and innuendo, no hard facts. Now of course speculation was rife as to how the soldiers would deal with him.

'He will work with them, of course, yes,' Claudia said gloomily at the breakfast table. 'It is only corruption, corruption.'

'No,' Jorge said. 'They will arrest him, they will take him away. It is obvious.'

Variations on these two points of view were repeated by everybody, from the kitchen staff to the casual patrons at Mama's place.

'What do you think?' Laurence said. The presence of the Brigadier had impressed itself on his psyche often enough to finally register there.

'I don't know,' I said. 'Let's wait and see.'

The truth was that I wasn't sure about any of the rumours surrounding the Brigadier. He was such a mythical figure by now that any scraps of idle talk stuck to him like facts. It was possible that he was just a lost and burnt-out piece of the past, not really here at all.

Not all of the speculation had to do with him. There was a sense that the arrival of the soldiers somehow marked a fresh life for the town. Rooms that were sealed up and empty were going to be occupied. Who knew what else might follow? Maybe shops would open, people would come, something at long last might happen.

But I couldn't see it. There were only three soldiers around the bar that first day; Mama had told me there might be three more. Six soldiers weren't going to make any difference to anything, but I didn't speculate about this either.

I went back on Thursday. Another four soldiers had arrived, and they were still awaiting the commander of the unit. But there would be a place for Laurence's girlfriend, Mama told me.

He was delighted. 'Thank you for organizing that, Frank.' He seemed to think that the room wouldn't have been available without me.

'What would you have done if there wasn't a place?'

He considered this soberly. 'Put off the visit, I guess.'

'You could've just shared your bed while I was here.'

'Oh, no. That wouldn't be right.'

He went down to Mama Mthembu's to see the room for himself. It was noisy, he told me, just above the courtyard, but fine. He put a vase of flowers, which he'd picked in the veld himself, on the table, as well as a framed photo of him and his girlfriend in the Sudan.

But his mood, late on that Thursday night, was melancholic and troubled. He seemed preoccupied with private thoughts.

'When did you last have a lover, Frank?' he asked me.

'Not since my marriage. Why are you asking? Are you worried about your girlfriend?'

'Well. You know. It's been a while since we saw each other. The last time was about a month before I came up here. I went to Lesotho to stay with her for a week.'

'And how was it?'

'Oh, that was wonderful. Great. Yes, we had a wonderful time.' But he spoke too forcefully, and avoided my eyes.

'You'll just have to see how it goes.'

'I was thinking of having a little party for her. Tomorrow night. Nothing too elaborate, just the people who work here. Would you come?'

'Me? Sure. Of course.'

It seemed a bizarre notion to me.

'Okay,' he said, his face warming a little. 'Say seven o'clock. That would be good, Frank. Thank you.'

I wouldn't have been able to avoid the party, because it happened in our room. When I got back from duty the gathering was already in full swing. I stood in the doorway, staring. It was an amazing picture. Everybody had come. Even Themba and Julius from the kitchen. Even Tehogo—who was there with the young man I'd seen hanging around, apparently his only friend. It was just Claudia, who'd taken over from me in the office, who wasn't there.

Nobody noticed me at first. Laurence had borrowed a music system from somewhere and a slightly stretched tape was playing too loudly. He'd filled several hospital bowls with peanuts and stale crisps, and bought a few litres of cheap boxed wine. Some kind of coloured plastic was tied around the light and in the lurid yellow glow people were sitting around and talking with uneasy jollity.

'Frank! Where were you? I thought you'd run away!' Laurence was very tense. He had a sort of desperate brightness as he came to get me at the door. 'Come and meet Zanele, I've been wanting to introduce you.'

I'd already noticed her from the doorway, standing rigidly in a corner, holding a glass of wine. She was small and pretty, with braided hair, wearing a bright West African dress; when she shook my hand I could feel the tension communicated through her long, thin fingers.

'Oh, hello,' she said, 'yes, Frank, yes.'

The American accent, in this room of flat vowels, was startling. And it was a shock to realize, after all the occasions when she'd been mentioned, that she wasn't African. I didn't know what to say and after an awkward moment I moved away. I'd seen Dr Ngema when I came in, perched unhappily on the edge of my bed, sipping from her glass and sneaking glances at her watch, and I went to sit next to her now; she turned to me with relief.

The first thing she said was, 'Frank, I've got to go in a moment.'

'Oh. All right.'

'I've got lots of work to do. But it's a lovely party, lovely.'

She said it with such insincere emphasis that I realized she thought I'd organized it.

'This is Laurence's party,' I said. 'Nothing to do with me.'

'Yes, yes. We should have little get-togethers more often. It's good for . . . for morale. Which reminds me, Frank. I wanted to ask you. In connection with your idea.'

'What idea?'

'Well, you know. The project. The outreach thing.' She dropped her voice in a secretive way. 'Laurence has talked to me. But I want to know: how did you know where to go?'

'What? I'm not with you, Ruth.'

'I mean, why that particular community? I didn't know you were interested in community work, Frank. You kept that very quiet.'

I stared at her, my head whirring. But the beginning of comprehension had started. I said, 'Did he tell you . . .'

'Shh. Shh.' She hissed it urgently at me. I broke off as Laurence came up to ask if we wanted more wine. 'No, thanks,' she said to him, 'I have to go in a moment.'

'So soon?'

'Work, work.' When he'd gone she turned quickly back to me. 'This isn't the moment to talk about it, Frank. But come and speak to me, all right? I've got some views on it.'

'Okay.'

'I'm not sure about the idea, Frank, to be honest. I don't think it'll work . . . I like change and innovation, you know that. But it's how you change. Or in this case, when. That's what matters. But here he comes, so shh. But talk to me soon, all right?' She drained her glass and set it down on the floor. 'Now I'd better go. Work, work. The office is calling me. But it's been a lovely party, Frank. Thank you so much.'

'It isn't my party,' I said again, but she was already on her way to the door.

Laurence hurried up with a glass of wine for me; he sat down on the bed. 'Did she have a good time? Dr Ngema? She didn't stay long.'

'Laurence, she said something I don't understand.'

'What?' He looked around at the awkward cheeriness in the room, which felt, like the tape, slightly stretched. 'Is this music all right, do you think?'

'It's fine.'

'Are you sure? And the party? Is everyone having a good time? Is it okay?'

'It's okay, Laurence.' But when I looked around, the peculiarity of the scene struck me again: Zanele talking to Jorge in the corner, Tehogo on the bed opposite me, an arm draped around the shoulder of his friend, and, in a space near the bathroom door, Themba and Julius dancing together. I almost didn't know where I was.

'Really? I wanted to do something to make Zanele feel, you know, welcome.'

'She looks happy.'

'Does she? But she always looks like that. She's a happy person.'

She did look a little more relaxed, nodding as she listened to Jorge. It was from Laurence, staring across at her with his wide, alarmed eyes, that the unhappiness seemed to come.

'You didn't tell me she's American.'

'Didn't I? Where did you think she came from?'

'The Sudan, obviously.'

'Sudan?' he said, amazed. 'No, no, she's from the States. I wanted to ask you,' he went on, in an offhand way, 'if you could do me a little favour.'

'What's that?'

'Do you think you could hang out with her for a couple of hours tomorrow night? I'm on duty, I don't want her to be alone.'

'Urn, yes, sure, I could do that. But if you speak to Dr Ngema, she could change your shift.'

'No, no, it's okay.'

'But she's come up here to see you. Don't you want to—'

'No, no, my shift is a commitment. I don't want to change it.'

In the past few weeks Dr Ngema had taken to giving Laurence shifts of duty on his own. He was absurdly proud of this change in status. But in truth he was only manning the office as a front; if any serious case came in, he had to call one of us. Nothing would be easier than for him to change his shift.

'She doesn't want me to change it, anyway,' he said.

'Who doesn't?'

'Zanele. Work comes first for both of us. And I'll see her on Sunday. Thanks for this, Frank. I appreciate it.'

Maybe Laurence's desperation had infected me, but I found myself getting very drunk very quickly. I downed glass after glass of wine, till at some point in the evening the merriment around me felt suddenly genuine. And I was part of it.

The configuration of bodies in the room had changed now. Themba and Julius were sitting on my bed. Claudia had somehow appeared while Jorge had gone, and she was locked in earnest conversation with Zanele and Laurence on the floor. I was sitting on the other bed, between Tehogo and his friend.

Tehogo's friend was called Raymond and his name felt comfortably familiar to me, so I must have been sitting there for a while. I'd seen him around often before, but we'd never exchanged more than a few terse words. He was young and almost girlishly pretty, with a smooth plastic skin and a charming smile. He had the same slick sense of style as Tehogo, so that with their short hair and gold jewellery and trendy city clothes neither of them seemed to belong here. The friendliness between the three of us also felt misplaced, unreal. Tehogo and I had hardly done more than grunt at each other, but there was a free flow of conversation tonight, which seemed to have risen up from nowhere. And we were sitting close to each other, so close that our shared body warmth was too hot, and Raymond had one elbow resting on my shoulder. Both of them were wearing their dark glasses, even in the under-lit room, giving a curious impression of blindness.

We were talking about me sharing a room with Laurence. How we had got on to this topic I have no idea, but I found myself announcing suddenly that I had wanted Tehogo's room.

His smile froze as he understood. Immediately I had to explain and justify: 'But no problem now. I don't want it any more.'

'You want my room?'

'No, no. I'm happy now. I talked to Dr Ngema about it once, but no problem any more. Really.'

Raymond said something to him and they both burst out laughing. Then Raymond said to me, 'You want his room, you wait.'

'No, no, I'm telling you, I don't want it.'

'One month, two month,' Raymond said. 'You wait.'

'You don't understand,' I started saying, then I thought about it. 'What's happening in two months?'

'He's getting a new job,' Raymond said.

'Is he?'

'New job,' Tehogo said. 'Good job.'

'What job?' I said. 'You can tell me. I'll keep it a secret.'

'Good work, bad work,' Raymond said. 'It's a good-bad job.'

Tehogo patted me reassuringly on the back. 'Don't worry. You stay here. You take my room. Then I come and cut off your head.'

They both laughed uproariously again. Then they spoke together across me and a more sober mood descended.

'This is joking talk,' Raymond said.

'No job,' Tehogo assured me. 'Everything is joking talk.'

Before I could speak again Laurence ducked anxiously into view. 'I'm worried about this music, Frank. Is the music okay?'

'Don't worry about the music'

But Tehogo overruled me. 'The music is no good,' he announced sternly. 'I have better music. Wait. Two minutes. I'm coming now.' He went out to get it. While he was gone Raymond kept leaning on me, talking into my ear. He was saying something about Laurence's girlfriend that I couldn't quite hear, but the tone was genial and insinuating; it sounded as if it might be funny, if I could catch it.

Then Tehogo was back with a handful of loose cassettes that he spilled over the floor. And the beat changed, becoming faster, more mindless and energetic, and somehow everybody was dancing. Everyone except Laurence. He sat on my bed and watched us with a puzzled, mournful expression. I called to him to join us, but he shook his head.

I was amazed at myself. I hadn't danced, I think, since my wedding. But now I found myself weaving and bouncing opposite the most unlikely of partners, Tehogo. And I didn't recognize in him the locked, earthbound body he slouched around in all day; he could really move. He was sinuous and supple, but strangest of all, he was happy. His grinning, sweating face seemed mad to me, till I recognized in it a mirror image of my own.

Something had happened to us that night; it was as if we'd fallen through a wall that normally bricked us in too tightly to move. The room opened and closed like a lurid flower around me. I wasn't myself. The loose abandon that had come over me was something foreign and lush. I felt as if I was up on a height, from which I could look down on the usual contours of my life and see how narrow and constricted they were. But I would never go back. I knew that all of us would stay where we were, in this high place, in this benevolent state of friendship that had fallen like grace upon us.

And then everyone was leaving. The music was played out, the wine was finished, and Tehogo and Raymond wanted me to go with them to Mama Mthembu's for more dancing and drinking. But I knew that I was done for the night. My head was already tender. I stood at the door, saying goodbye to everybody, as if I was the host and they were all my invited guests.

'See you in the morning,' I said to Tehogo. I enfolded him in an embrace, feeling his thin shoulder-blades moving under my hands.

'Remember,' Raymond said. 'In two months you can have your own room.'

'He is joking,' Tehogo said. 'It is not true.'

'I don't know what's true any more,' I said.

More laughter, rootless and excessive. Then the place was emptied out. In the weak light of the lamp I recognized my room again, full of rubbish and rubble. From the speakers came an endless soft crackle of static.

'I'm just taking Zanele home,' Laurence said. 'I'll be back in a minute.'

She was smiling self-consciously, tucking a strand of hair behind one ear. She didn't look at me.

'Come back in the morning.'

'Oh, I wouldn't leave you with all this to clear up. That's not fair.'

'We can do it tomorrow.'

'No, no. I'll be back in a minute.'

When they were gone I contemplated the debris and skewed furniture while the buoyancy in me started to flatten out. I couldn't believe that I'd danced and drunk like somebody half my age, but the youthfulness felt good, and from its gassy glow it was Laurence Waters who looked old and tired and jaded. Why wasn't he spending the night with her?

He was back in fifteen minutes or so. Though he'd said he was coming back to clean up, he only looked at the disorder of the room and sank on to his bed. 'Was that all right?' he said.

'How do you mean?'

'The party. Was it okay? Did people enjoy it?'

'I think so.'

'Really? How did it compare with other parties?'

'Laurence, in all the years I've been here, nobody's ever had a party. Yours was the first.'

'Really?' he said again. A dim smile broke through the anxiety. 'You were fantastic, Frank.'

'That's because I'm drunk.'

'Are you?'

'I'm so drunk, Laurence. Jesus Christ. It's been years since I felt like this.'

'Oh, good, good,' he said vaguely. His face clouded again. 'But why did Dr Ngema leave early?'

'I don't think parties are her thing.'

He nodded distractedly and made a show of collecting some paper cups together. I watched him for a while, then I said: 'What's this outreach project she was talking about?'

'Oh, that.'

'Well, what is it?'

'You should know, Frank. You're the first person I told about it.'

'Your travelling clinic'

He nodded. 'But I must thank you. It was your idea that I try Maria's village first. It was a great suggestion.'

'You've been to Maria's village?'

'A few times. It's ideal. So the plan is to hold a trial clinic there in a week or so. See how it goes. And if it's successful . . .' He laughed. 'No more symbols, Frank. You were right.'

'Why has nobody said a word about it?'

'Dr Ngema's going to tell everybody at the staff meeting on Monday. Let's not talk about it now, Frank. I'm not in the mood.'

So we let the subject drop and soon afterwards we fell asleep. It bothered me that this project had taken shape at Maria's village without anybody telling me, but it was part of the weird harmony of the evening that it also didn't matter. The past was complex and fractured, but it was past. Tomorrow was another day.

I woke in the morning with a terrible headache suspended between my temples. We had left the lamp on and its wan glow mixed with daylight to reveal the mess in the room. Crisps trodden into the floor, broken plastic cups holding the dregs of wine.

When I got up I saw that somebody had knocked the wooden fish that Laurence had given me off the table; it lay broken on the floor. I threw the pieces into the bin and peered through my pain at Laurence sprawled face-down, his mouth open, a string of saliva on his lip. The day already had a used and ugly look to me.

A hot shower and an aspirin didn't help. Laurence was still asleep when I went out. I wasn't sure yet where I was going, but I just wanted to get away.

As I emerged into the corridor, Tehogo was locking his door. He seemed in as much pain as me. I knew I ought to smile at him, but the smile just wasn't in me this morning.

He said to me, 'My tapes.'

'What?'

'You've got my tapes. In your room.'

It took a moment for my blurred brain to understand. Then his rudeness irritated me. 'Laurence is still sleeping,' I said shortly. 'You can get them later.'

He grunted and in an instant it was there with us again: all the dourness and sourness and mistrust. The past, recharged and renewed. Nothing was different after all.

I carried this with me all day. The headache didn't lift and my mind felt crazed through with thin lines of unease. I was thinking, not very coherently, about Laurence and his girlfriend and the party. I knew I had undertaken to spend some time with Zanele tonight, but the reason wasn't clear to me any more. I was resentful at being entangled in Laurence's personal affairs and it felt to me that if I stayed away, on my own, for long enough, my obligation would fade.

But it didn't fade. When I went back in the late afternoon he was busy cleaning up the room. The first thing he said was, 'Oh, thank God. I thought you'd run out on me.'

'Laurence, listen. Let me do your duty for you. Then you can—'

'No, no, forget it. I told you, it's a commitment.'

I lay and watched him, toiling on his hands and knees, a wet cloth in his hand. There were stains on the floor that would never come out.

9

I arrived late and she was waiting downstairs for me, wearing another of those West African suits. She had a touch of makeup on and I saw that she'd taken some trouble to look good. But I was in the same clothes I'd worn all day, with two days' growth of beard and a dull pain behind my eyes.

We had to eat at Mama's place; there was nowhere else in town. So I led her through. The bar was full. From the haircuts and attitude I recognized the full contingent of soldiers, a group mixed in race and age. But there were also more of the other regulars than usual, the scattering of clerks and farmers and workers that were the motley population of the town. There was a table open in the courtyard, by chance the very same one I'd sat at with Laurence the first day, in the corner under the bougainvillaea. Mama came over to serve us and I ordered whisky.

'Is that a good idea?' Zanele said.

'Hair of the dog. I couldn't get by without anaesthetic. And there's nowhere else to find it in this whole godforsaken place.'

She smiled. 'It is kind of a strange spot. Not what I was expecting, I guess.'

'What were you expecting?'

'Well, Laurence didn't say . . . in his letters . . . I had a different idea.'

I don't know what her different idea was. But I could see that the place made her uneasy: she kept looking around distractedly. I didn't want to be here myself, but I made an effort to shed my burden of bad grace. It wasn't so unpleasant sitting opposite a pretty face, whisky in hand.

Things mellowed once I'd had a bit to drink. We talked about this and that—her background, how she'd landed up out here. She came from middle America somewhere, the daughter and grand-daughter of black Americans. There was nothing African about her, really—not even her name. Zanele was a name she took on when she came out to the Sudan. Her real name, it turned out, was Linda.

'Linda's a nice name,' I said.

But she shook her head. She wanted to leave it all behind, that middle-class childhood of half-privilege and displaced values. She thought she was African now, but she had the manner and confidence of another continent completely.

Still, there was something about her mission I admired. She was actually out here, slogging in the Sudanese desert, roughing it in the Drakensberg mountains. She told me about her life in Lesotho, and none of it made me envious. I was on to my third whisky, feeling good now, and I ordered another along with my food. It was easy to listen, while she talked about a library, a crèche, a literacy training programme, even a village bank—all of this started and run by the people of an impoverished community in the high mountains. With the help of overseas funding, which she'd helped to raise. It sounded utopian—and of course it was: none of this had really come to pass yet, it was all in the pipeline. Meanwhile she and six other foreign volunteers were sleeping on mattresses on the floor, while the days passed in grubby work that ranged from inoculating cattle to digging irrigation ditches.

'And you? What are you doing there?'

'I'm a teacher. The only one in the village. I teach children of all different ages—six to sixteen.'

'What do you teach them?'

'Different subjects. Math, English. Some history.'

'Can't be too effective.'

'Why not?'

'Well, I mean. Different ages all together. Different levels. All those subjects.'

'It's not like the schools you probably went to,' she said, a bit stiffly. 'But it does have some effect. These are very poor people. Anything is better than nothing.'

'Is it?'

'Well, of course. Don't you think so?'

'It seems to me,' I said, 'that past a certain point, anything is exactly the same as nothing.'

She was watching me warily. 'Have you ever done it?'

'What? Gone to do volunteer work with a poor community somewhere? No. Maybe I don't believe in it. Or maybe this place is it.'

'No,' she said. 'This place isn't it. What you're doing here isn't community work. You don't know what you're talking about.'

She and Laurence were the same kind of person: blindly and naïvely believing in their own power to change things. It was simple, this belief, and the simplicity was strong and foolish. I could see how they might have been drawn to each other, up at the camp in Sudan—Laurence the young healer, earnest and passionate, she the lost seeker with her new name. And how South Africa, down at the bottom end of the continent, with its glorious future just beginning, might have seemed like a backdrop to their belief.

But that was only part of it, of course. Because I could also see how mismatched they were. Behind the brave aspirations, what did these two really have in common? Their relationship was just another idea—dry and sensible, like everything they did. And they had started to realize it too. Which is why she and I were sitting at this table now, while Laurence was a kilometre away, doing a shift of duty he didn't need to do.

Talk turned inevitably to Laurence. She said, 'I wanted to thank you for looking after him. He's mentioned you in every single letter. It's helped him a lot to have you here.'

'I haven't helped him.'

'Well, he thinks you have. Maybe you don't know this, but Laurence doesn't have friends. You're the first friend he's ever made. It's important to him.'

'Why doesn't Laurence have friends?'

'I don't know. Maybe he's too preoccupied. He is a touch wrapped up in himself. Of course, you know his background.'

'Some of it. Not too much. I know about his parents being killed.'

'His parents?' She stared at me. 'That's not right.'

'Weren't his mother and father killed in an accident?'

She shook her head and looked at the table. 'That's an old story,' she said. 'I don't know why he told you that. I thought he'd got over it.'

'So what's the truth?'

'His parents aren't dead. He's an illegitimate child. His father wasn't ever around. His mother raised him on her own. But she told him that story about his parents dying, and how she'd taken over—'

'That she was his sister.'

'Right. That story.'

I felt somehow betrayed. 'He told me a long saga about looking for their graves one day . . .'

'Well, that part is true. He did go looking for them. That was when his sister—his mother—came out with it and told him the truth. It was a big thing for him. But it's all history now. I don't know why he lied to you.'

'As dark secrets go,' I said, 'that's pretty disappointing. It's not the Middle Ages any more.'

She looked troubled; it gave her face an added depth. It was on the tip of my tongue to say something reckless, but at that moment Mama arrived with our food. I transferred my attention reluctantly. 'Full house tonight,' I said.

'Everybody's here,' Mama said. She couldn't seem to stop smiling, all her good fortune radiating from the gap between her front teeth. Her plump arms, as she set down our plates, gave off a jangling of bracelets that was like the sound of cash in a drawer.

'All the soldiers have arrived?'

'Even the boss. Colonel Moller. He came yesterday.'

'Who?' I said.

It was like a hot light growing in my head.

'Colonel Moller. Ooh, such a nice man. That's him there inside, by the bar. You want more ice with that drink?'

'No, thanks.' I'd started to sweat. It was too much, surely; too much of a coincidence. But I had to see for myself. I went to the bathroom to wash my hands. The figure that Mama had indicated was at the far end of the bar and it was only on the way back that I could stare into his face for two long seconds. Yes, it was him; not much different, despite the ten intervening years. He was a little slacker and older; he'd gained one rank and was in charge of a mixed group of soldiers—black and white together, some of them the enemy he'd been trying to kill. His life must feel very different to him, sent up here on this unlikely posting, but to me he was the same, unchanged. The narrow, fanatical features, the lean body generating a disproportionate power. He stared back at me with dead eyes, then looked away. He didn't know who I was.

I found that I was trembling. Zanele looked curiously at me as I settled myself again. 'What's the matter?'

'Oh, nothing. I'm all right.'

But I wasn't all right. My mind was knotted up with what it had seen. I sat and picked at my food, but I wasn't in the room any more. I was following the brown back of a corporal through the dark, towards a lighted cell . . . and then stumbling away again, alone.

I shook my head to rid it of the memory. But though the room came back to me, with all its new chatter and activity, something was different now. Something in me, perhaps, but it found its way into the silence at our table.

Eventually I put my fork down. I said, 'That man in there, by the bar. He was someone I worked under in the army.'

But she didn't even look into the bar. She stared at me and said, 'You were in the army?'

And I could see what this meant to her. The army, the bad old days: she was having dinner with an enemy.

I said defensively, 'Laurence told me he was sorry he'd missed the army. He said he thought it was a formative experience.'

'Laurence says silly things sometimes. He doesn't know how the world works.'

'But he's got a point. A year of community service up here isn't going to teach him much. He might've been better off in a shit-hole in the bush. Let him kill people, let people try to kill him. Then we'd see. He wouldn't talk about country clinics and helping the human race any more.'

I was surprised at my own anger, the coldness and clearness of it—though I wasn't sure who it was directed at. We were in a world without nuances now, in which all the subtle gradations of colour had turned into black and white.

She pushed her chair back from the table. 'Don't,' she said. 'Don't talk like that.'

But I was unstoppable by now. 'Why? Is that too real for you? Ideas are always better than reality, of course. But sooner or later the real world always wins. Laurence will find that out. So will you, when you go back to America and lose your African outfits and your fake name.'

'Fuck you, mister.'

'The feeling is mutual,' I said, as she stood up and stalked out. I sat crunching an ice-cube, reflecting on how quickly it had all gone off the rails. My cold anger went on burning for a while. But it wasn't her I was thinking about; it was Laurence. And I remember that his name, Laurence Waters, seemed suddenly like a combination of blandness and intrigue, banality and piety, that offended me.

*   *   *

It didn't take long for me to calm down. And then I wasn't so proud of myself any more. I got a tray from Mama, set our plates and glasses on it and climbed the stairs. But she wouldn't answer when I knocked, though the silence behind the door was charged.

'Please,' I said. 'I was totally out of line. I'm really sorry. I'm drunk. I had no right.'

'Fuck off,' she eventually told me.

'I can't. I can't go back and tell Laurence I insulted you.'

'I don't care. I don't care about you or Laurence. The two of you are obviously in love with each other, so why don't both of you just fuck off.'

It was maybe the first time in years that I was speechless. Something of my amazement must have carried through the door, because in the ensuing silence I heard the bolt slide back.

It took me a moment to get myself together. I picked up the tray from the floor where I'd put it and went in. The room was in darkness, the only light from the courtyard outside. I remembered at a glance, from when I'd stayed here, the frugal furnishings: the narrow single bed, the table with two chairs, the sink in the corner. She was sitting at the table, by the window, looking curiously set and formal. I went over and put the tray down.

'Well,' I said at last.

'I'm sorry.'

'Aren't we two having a fine time.'

'I'm very mixed up,' she said. 'Confused and angry. It's all over, isn't it—me and Laurence. If it ever really happened.'

I sat down opposite her. There didn't seem to be anything to say. The whole evening was just a jumbled mess of emotions with no clear focus in the middle. The sound of voices and laughter carried up from outside. On the table was the photograph of her and Laurence in the desert, both smiling into the camera. I picked it up and tilted it towards the dim light coming in through the window.

'You guys look happy here,' I said.

'That's because we were working. He's happy when he's working. But I don't make him happy.'

'Does he make you happy?'

'I don't know. I guess not. I can't remember.'

'Why don't you eat your food,' I said, like a mother.

'I'm not hungry. I'm fucked-up. I'm sorry.'

'It's all right. I'm sorry too. We're all sorry.'

She was bitter, but all the fight had gone out of her. She was slumped and sad in the chair, like a windless sail. In the silence I could hear her breathing. Suddenly, on a fresh impulse, she said, 'Let's get out of here. It's so . . . stuffy.'

'But where will we go?'

'I don't know. There must be somewhere.'

'Not really. We could take a drive.'

'It seems kind of desperate.'

'But we are.'

She gave a small, unhappy laugh. 'What's that place there,' she said, 'that big place on the hill?'

I'd been looking at it too, like a gothic galleon stranded by a flood.

'That's the Brigadier's house.'

'Who's the Brigadier?'

'The Brigadier is the ex-tinpot dictator of the ex-homeland. The capital of which is where we are.'

'And where is he now, this Brigadier?'

'Well,' I said, 'that is the question. It depends who you listen to. Some people think he's dead and gone. Other people say he's around, running refugees and stolen goods and arms and stuff back and forth over the border. His retirement job, you could call it. These guys, the soldiers, are here to plug up the holes. Supposedly. But all of it's just talk talk talk. Who knows what's real?'

'What do you think?'

'Well, you can see what I'm like. Always ready to believe the worst. Keeps me prepared for all eventualities.'

'Have you ever seen him?'

'Oh, *ja*. In the old days he was always around. I saw him here once, as a matter of fact.'

'Here?'

'Well, down there. In the courtyard. I came here for a drink and there were all these security goons standing around. They only let me as far as the bar. The rest of it was closed off. I could see him through the door, eating with his wife. Little man. But I had a closer encounter than that.'

'When was that?'

'When he came to the hospital while I was on duty. He had chest pains, he said. The security guys were all over the place. I called Dr Ngema and she came to look after him. But in the meanwhile I listened to his heart through my stethoscope, so I can confirm that it does actually beat.'

She was fascinated. 'How did he treat you?'

'Polite but distant. I don't think he noticed me much. He was worried about his chest pains.'

'And what were they?'

'Bad conscience? Gas? I don't know. Dr Ngema took care of it and he went away.'

The memory of this event was suddenly strong again: the tiny shirtless man on the edge of the bed, holding his military cap in his hands. He was very stiff and upright, very neat.

'Were you afraid?'

I had to think for a moment. 'Yes, I suppose I was. I tend to be afraid of what can kill me, even if it's not likely to happen.'

'Incredible.' She turned her serious, excited face to me, and I knew it before she spoke. It was as if all the turmoil of the evening had led to this single, clarifying idea. 'Let's go there.'

'Where?'

'To his house.'

'He doesn't live there any more. It's empty.'

'It doesn't matter, I want to see. Let's just take a look.'

'All right,' I said. I was glad to have found something to distract her. I wanted to make her happy.

So we drove towards the bright mansion on the hill. It was lit up every night, even though it was empty; some lackey or watchman throwing a switch. Keeping the old symbols shining.

There was only one road to the top. I imagine it had been made at the same time as the house was built; nobody else lived up here. The view was impressive. I'd been there only once or twice before, and that was soon after I'd arrived in the town. On the last occasion there'd been a very unpleasant incident. I'd parked and was sitting, looking out, when a policeman came and knocked on the window. I was forced to get out of the car. I had to lean on the bonnet while he searched me. Then another policeman arrived and they started to push me around. Not badly, but enough to get me scared. They were both young and full of impassive enmity. I remember that an image came to me of my wife reading an article on the third page of a city newspaper: *Doctor vanishes in bantustan.* And that would be that.

But then an officer appeared and everything cooled down. He was polite and professional with me. I shouldn't come up the hill, he said; the Brigadier had many enemies and the police and army had been told to take no chances. There were other hills, he said, pointing out into the distance, from which to admire the view.

This would have been an innocuous ending to a potentially nasty story, except that there'd been a subsequent instalment. The first policeman, who'd shown such exemplary qualities of brutishness, was someone I'd never seen before and hoped never to see again; but six months later he was personally appointed by the Brigadier as chief of police in the town. It was indicative of something that he'd been promoted over the head of the kindly officer who'd saved me, and who turned out to be the man I would never see again.

I hadn't been back, even though these days the hilltop wasn't out of bounds any more. There were two other cars parked up here, discreet and dark—lovers, I supposed, come from who knows where for a bit of late—night fumbling—and I stopped a little way from them. The valley was a mesh of lights below us. From this height the town seemed ordinary; the same as any other country town at night. It would take a close scrutiny and a sharp brain to see that there were no moving headlamps and that most of the windows were dark.

'Could we take a walk around it?' The view didn't interest her; she only had eyes for the house. But all you could see were high walls topped with barbed wire and a roof on the other side.

'We can't go in.'

'I know, but let's take a look from outside.'

The main entrance in front had a pair of steel doors on rollers. We pressed our eyes to the join, but there was only the thinnest slice of a view: grass and a pillar and steps. I thought I could see a sentry-box. We walked around the corner and down the side. And came to a stop.

'Frank,' she said. 'I don't believe it.'

I couldn't believe it either. A small side gate, set into the wall. Ajar and open. Inside, barely visible, the gloomy spaces of a garden.

'It doesn't mean we have to go through,' I said.

'Who left it open?'

'I don't know. A worker, maybe. Or a security guard. With a gun.'

'Oh, come on. We're not going to steal anything.'

'I don't think this is a good idea,' I said.

But she went in and after a minute I followed her. I found myself in a quiet cul-de-sac off the main route of the garden. There was no light here, but as I moved further in the dark screens of leaves composed themselves into hedges. There was a loose crunching of gravel and twigs under my feet, which sounded terrifyingly loud to me. I tried to tread carefully, holding my breath, but let out a little cry of alarm as I lurched against her in the blackness. She giggled and clutched at me, a warm embrace that slid immediately away.

'What're you so afraid of?' she whispered.

'We're not supposed to be here.'

'We're just taking a look.'

I followed as she moved away towards the wash of light higher up. The house came into view, big and gleaming and solid. We had entered into what must have been the bottom of the garden, and were moving towards a central avenue. A slate path led to a lawn with a sundial. Beyond it there was a gravel road, with flowerbeds and separate grottoes off on the other side, and I glimpsed what looked like a putting green.

The grounds were big, an acre or two, and elaborate. But as we moved closer to the light I could see that the gardens, although they were ragged and turning brown in places, were not completely neglected. The shapes in the topiary were blurred but still visible and the lawn wasn't overly long. Somebody was keeping an eye. And maybe this wasn't so absurd: some new politician with a new function would be posted here some time. I remembered the abandoned house near the river. This wasn't the same. This was a different kind of desertion. People hadn't left here completely; it was only history that had temporarily vacated its shell, until it could take up office once more in a different shape.

She'd stopped walking again. I caught up with her and started to speak, but she held up a hand to quieten me. And when I stopped I could hear it too.

It seemed incredible: voices in the garden. Two of them, speaking back and forth, in a murmur too low for individual words to be distinct. I strained my ears to hear what was being said. But instead two different sounds started up, which I recognized, but couldn't believe. Not here, so late at night. But the sounds went on, and there was no doubt about them.

It was absurd. We were listening to a lawnmower—one of those outmoded manual mowers—and a pair of shears. The soft noise of this bizarre industry in the dark was like another language, as clear and incomprehensible as the two voices. It was hard to tell where exactly the activity was happening, but it seemed to be behind the wall of foliage next to us. The clack-clack of the shears was steady, but the mower was going up and down, up and down, and when it reached the end of its circuit we could hear the voice of the man pushing it, fixed perpetually on a note of complaint.

I touched Zanele's arm and gestured. Although I wasn't afraid any more and the situation was almost ridiculous, I wouldn't want to show myself to the gardeners. To go any closer to the house would be to step into full view in the light, so we retreated down the alley on the other side. As we moved away, the urge grew in me to laugh. Our transgression was a childish one, not dangerous after all, but when I turned to her to speak I saw one of the statues in the garden, of which there were many, randomly arranged, break into calm motion and step sedately towards us. And in an instant all the danger in the world was alive and possible again.

We had both frozen, waiting. The statue came ambling into our path, until a strip of light from the house revealed the peaked cap and uniform of the security guard I'd imagined.

'We didn't mean to trespass,' I said.

'The gate was open,' she said, 'so we came to take a look.'

'We came to look,' I repeated. We were talking fast, overlapping each other, but our nervousness didn't touch him. He was standing quite still, considering us. Then he rocked on his feet, out of shadow into the light and out again, but in that brief second I knew who he was.

The Brigadier wasn't a brigadier. Until he staged his coup he was just an ordinary captain in the homeland defence force. Nobody had heard of him before. And it could only have been with the help of bigger, unseen friends that he had emerged from the shadows with such sudden support and power. After he had appointed himself chief minister he heaped numerous honours on his own shoulders, including his rank and a handful of medals. He was wearing the rank and the medals now, although officially both the uniform and the army it belonged to didn't exist any more. He made a soft clinking noise when he moved.

He said, 'I opened the gate.'

I remembered the voice. Cool, flat, soft. It was far more distinctive than his face, which was small and ordinary. His voice was memorable. I had heard it coming out of the radio and television, always level and void of feeling, no matter what it was saying. You remembered the even, dead tone, though you might not hear the words.

What did he say, in those few brief years when he was playing god over his little artificial world? I couldn't tell you one quote or original line. No, it was the usual rhetoric about self-determination and a bright future, scripted for him no doubt by his white masters elsewhere. Pretoria had put: him in power when his predecessor started to get troublesome, even though he was far more venal and corrupt. And he knew what he had to do to stay in place.

But the timing was bad. If the political scene had stayed on track he might've been able to proclaim himself life-president and people's hero for the next forty years. But not too long after he took over, the white government down in the real capital gave in and power started to change hands. And two or three years later he was out of a job. And a few years on from that, here he was, dressed up for his role in the middle of the night, preening around the empty set with two bit players in the background.

I said to Zanele, 'Do you know who this is?'

She shook her head.

'This is the Brigadier.'

'This?'

'Yes.'

We both stared at him. The conversation we'd just had wouldn't have been conceivable a few years ago. We'd spoken contemptuously about him, as if he wasn't there. And now we were looking at him in the interested way you might look at an object. But he was unperturbed. He stood, rocking on his heels, no expression on that tiny, stolid face. His eyes glinted whitely in the gloom.

But now she changed. Since I'd started describing him to her, much earlier in the evening, I'd been aware that her fascination contained an element that was disturbingly close to arousal. Now you could see it happen. It was as if she'd been introduced to a celebrity. Something in her warmed and opened to him; she looked at him differently; she actually moved closer.

'We wanted to see your house,' she said.

'You want to see my house?'

'Yes.'

'Come.'

He started walking back the way we'd come, giving off that clink of metal. She looked quickly at me, almost guiltily, then followed. I hung back for a moment, and only caught up where they'd stopped next to the two men working in the garden.

The men looked as strange as they'd sounded. They were both dressed in brown military overalls that were too big for them. One man was white, a few years older than me, with thinning ginger hair and a swollen, florid face I recognized from newspaper photographs; he was one of the 'advisers' that the white government had assigned to the homeland cabinet, back in the days of the first deposed chief minister. He'd come a long way, through a military coup and the annulment of all his labour, to end up pushing a lawnmower at midnight. The other man was young and black and fresh-faced; I didn't know him. They were both staring at us in bemusement, while the Brigadier spoke to them in a low voice. He told them to move on to the next area of the garden; he was just going up to the house and would be back in a moment. Then he set off again, dragging us behind him, up the long central avenue and the broad back steps to the slate stoep. Through French doors there was a glimpse of a dark room, emptied of furniture.

The house was large, ostentatiously designed, but otherwise there was nothing remarkable about it. In a big city it would've been merely one of many sumptuous, tasteless houses. What made it striking here was its lonely setting on the top of a brown hill, with a green moat of garden around it. But now that we were standing here, up close, I wondered what we were looking at.

'Did they take everything away?' Zanele said.

He nodded sadly. 'Everything. They came with three trucks.'

'Where did they take it?'

He shrugged. 'To Pretoria. They said they wanted to look after it. But by now where is it all?' He nodded meaningfully. 'Gone. Gone.'

We could see him now in the light. And though he was clean-shaven and gave off a hint of perfume from somewhere, there was a dissolution in his face. A crassness, an undoing of the muscles from deep inside. His eyelids hung heavily down.

But she didn't notice. Though she didn't touch him it was as though she'd put a hand on his arm. And I saw that I was wrong to think that his power had been taken from him. He was still a dangerous man, as dangerous as anybody who will do anything he wants to you in a locked room somewhere, and he gave off his power like the metallic smell of sex.

Leaning to him, she said, 'Can we, could we, go in?'

'They took the keys. They changed the locks. They threw me out of my own house.'

'How did you open the garden gate?'

'That key I kept.' He smiled slowly. 'There is always one lock they forget to change.'

'Why are you looking after the garden?'

'Who else will do it? I ask you: who else? These people? They can take, but they can't give anything. So I come sometimes, once a week, twice a week, just to make everything okay.'

'It must be difficult for you. Lots of memories.'

'*Ja*,' he said. 'I remember everything. Everything.'

'Do you mind if we take a look around?'

'Come.'

He went ahead of her, like an official leading a guided tour. But there was nothing to see. Just one empty room after another, visible only through heavy glass and shrubbery. They went around the side, stopping to peer in every few steps. He pronounced the function of each room—'reception hall', 'pantry', 'study'—like a fact loaded with great historical significance. But he was outside the history now, looking in at it through a thin but impervious barrier.

When we had gone around to the front of the house, where the pillars and the sentry-box were, he paused at the top of the steps. From here there was a view of the town. 'If it was daytime,' he said, 'you could see my statue now.' He meant the one down there, at the crossroads. She came and stood next to him, staring down into the dark.

I didn't exist for them. Since our little walk had begun, he hadn't once looked at me. She was his sympathetic ear. And I felt for her a rising revulsion that was not unconnected with desire.

But it was true that the strangeness of the scene was powerful, inclining all attention towards the small, lost figure at its centre. The emptiness of the house seemed somehow to emanate from him. He gave off a melancholy, injured air, as if he'd been dispossessed of his birthright, instead of what he'd taken by force. And in this moment it was hard, even for me, to see him as truly dangerous. He was like a child dressed up for some imaginary role.

The front door was heavy; now he went and tried the handle as if he thought that this time, just once, it would open for him again. I was glad we couldn't go in. It would have been too much to follow this tiny monster through the entrails of his old domain. He stood like a shadow across the bright scene of the garden, in which the two figures were still moving, pruning and mowing. Beyond the wall the dead frieze of lights marked the town.

I said, 'We have to go.'

She heard the note in my voice. She shifted her weight uneasily and said, 'Well.'

But he had heard it too. For the first time he looked directly at me. From behind the ivory glint of his eyeballs I could feel his disdain. He said, 'Do you not like my house?'

'What do you come here for?'

'To look.'

'To look at what? This is past for you.'

The silence deepened and grew. She said again, 'Well.'

But he moved closer to me. 'What have they done with this place? Nothing. They throw me out, they take my furniture. Three trucks came. Three.' He held up three fingers. The number seemed important to him.

'It didn't belong to you.'

He ignored me. 'Then they leave it. They do nothing. If I don't take care of the garden, what will happen? It will die. Who will cut the grass? Who will give it water? If I don't guard everything, one day some rubbish will break in and live in these rooms. These beautiful rooms.'

She said anxiously, 'It must be hard for you.'

'It is hard. Very hard. One day to be living here. Next day living in a tent. One day everything is possible. Next day nothing is possible any more. Terrible. Terrible.' He turned his head heavily back to me. 'So tell me, Doctor, if you were me, would you not want to come back?'

Doctor: the word dropped coldly into me, like a stone: he knew.

'I don't know,' I said. 'I don't know what it's like to be you.'

He smiled slowly again, baring his big, white teeth. 'I will tell you. People, small people, nothing people, they think I am the past. But I am not the past. My time is coming still.'

'Good,' I said. 'I am very happy for you. But now we have to go. It's very late. Linda. I mean, Zanele.'

'Yes,' she said. 'Well. Thank you. It was nice to meet you.'

He took her hand and bowed over it, still wearing that big smile, like another worthless medal. I was already halfway down the steps.

She caught up with me as I was passing the two gardeners. They had moved on to a new section and were back in their rhythmic cycle of cutting and complaint. Their faces looked up in consternation as we went by; then the noise of clacking blades started up behind us again.

'Slow down,' she said. 'What's the hurry?'

I slowed. We walked in silence the whole way back—to the gate, then up the side of the house. We had to go past the other cars before we got to ours: a black one and a white one parked next to each other, like some crassly obvious symbol of unity. I'd thought they belonged to romantic lovers—arbitrary people visiting the hilltop—but now I knew their cargo was more sinister. I laughed aloud.

'What's so funny?'

'It isn't funny, actually.'

'What isn't funny?'

How could I explain? It all came down again to simple, unreal ideas. Earlier in the evening she had seen me as a villain because I'd told her I'd been in the army. And now this awful little man was some kind of icon to her, just because he'd been in charge. Never mind the homeland, the violence, the greed; never mind the dirty politics and meaningless titles. It was the clear moral universe that Laurence inhabited, in which no power was ever truly false.

'Nothing,' I said.

We coasted down the hill in silence, both staring in front of us, with the lights of the town rising. Then we were back among the deserted streets, the crumbling buildings. As I stopped outside Mama's place, I had a moment of dry-mouthed uncertainty: was the silence empty with failure, or heavy with possibility? But as I turned towards her I knew. She was turning towards me too. Our mouths locked hotly. And even then—before the climb up the stairs, the room with the hard little bed—all the echoes from the evening were with us, so that more than two people were grappling together there in the dark.

10

When I got back to the hospital that night I could see him inside the office—on duty, sitting at the desk. But although he must have heard my car pull in, he didn't come to the window to look. And I didn't go in to see him.

I didn't feel guilt; not then. The guilt came later, slowly, like a dark seed starting to sprout. What I felt that night was a kind of perverse closeness to him, as if an agreement had been fulfilled: as if the contract was between him and me, and she was the instrument.

I saw him the next morning when he came in. He looked tired and drawn, but he wasn't going to bed. He shaved and showered and dressed in clean clothes. Then he asked—but casually, in an offhand way—how last night had been.

'Oh, okay. We sat at Mama's and had dinner. Nothing too exciting.'

'Thanks for helping me, Frank. You're a real friend.'

I don't know why I said nothing about the Brigadier. That part of the evening didn't reflect on me. But when I saw her with Laurence a bit later, before she set out to drive back to Lesotho, I knew that she hadn't told him about it either. It was odd, but the angry intimacy of the end of the evening seemed to have begun in the forbidden garden on the hill.

'Thank you for keeping me company,' she said, holding out a hand. 'It was good to meet you.'

So formal, so nice. Her face was closed and neutral. I shook her hand, but our eyes didn't meet, and when the time came for her to leave I kept myself busy in the office.

Laurence went out with her. He was back five minutes later, looking thoughtful and preoccupied, but I could still feel him glancing at me from time to time. It was as though he could see the infidelity in my face. But my expression was calm and clean; I had learned with Claudia how to conceal betrayal.

By the time night came I knew what I wanted to do. I got into my car and drove through town to a telephone booth on the far side. There were other telephones I could've used, one right at the hospital, but somehow this lonely spot, at the very edge of things, was the most suitable place to hear her voice.

'I don't know why I'm calling,' I said.

'Who is this?'

'Cast your mind back. We're still married to each other, technically speaking.'

'Frank? Oh! Frank!'

She sounded so joyful that for a moment everything seemed possible again.

'Karen,' I said. 'You've been on my mind.'

'I've been thinking about you too, Frank. This is such a coincidence! I've been going to call you. To tell you that the agreement's ready now. You can come and sign it.'

My mind was so far from this subject that it took me a few seconds to understand that she was talking about our divorce agreement, the dissolution of our marriage.

'Yes,' I said. 'So you want me to come down there?'

'That doesn't seem so much to ask, Frank, after seven years, does it? Other people manage to do it without running away. For God's sake!'

Her querulous voice came shivering down the line to me out of the dark, out of the past. The telephone booth I was standing at was on the gravel verge of the last road, at the edge of the light. A step away from me the blackness began, and the bush. I could see serrated rows of leaves and hear the soft sibilance that came out of them: wind, branches, insects sending signals to each other. I said, 'You don't have to.'

'What?'

'Talk like this. You can have the divorce. I'm not running any more.'

There was a pause before she talked again, more conciliatory now, but wary. 'That's good, Frank. We have to, we have to let go now.'

'I'll come down in a few days.'

'When?'

'Can I let you know? I have to make some arrangements here—'

'Can't you at least give me some idea? We're trying to arrange our lives at this end too, you know.'

'Thursday,' I said. 'How about Thursday?'

'Thursday would be fine. I'll bring the agreement home.'

'All right. I'll see you then.'

'Frank. That wasn't what you were calling about. What were you calling about?'

I had to think about it until I remembered, and even then I wasn't completely sure what I'd been calling about. Just to hear her voice. But I wanted to hear it saying things it would never say again; they were lost, buried, gone. I put down the phone and stood there with my face pressed to the plastic rim of the booth, looking out into the dark. The past and the future are dangerous countries; I had been living in no man's land, between their borders, for the last seven years. Now I felt myself moving again, and I was afraid.

I got back into the car and drove slowly to Maria in her shack. But I didn't know what I was looking for there either. I was aimless and displaced. I sat down on a crate in the corner, rubbing at my forehead.

'Friday, Saturday, you don't come,' she said. 'Why, why?'

I was with Laurence's girlfriend. But I didn't say that. These were questions that belonged to a normal relationship; not here.

'I've been very busy. Working.'

'Working.'

'Yes.'

She was sitting apart from me, in the dark corner. The lamp was next to me, burning hotly.

'Tonight you come early. Why?'

It was six or seven—long before my usual visiting time. I hadn't even realized that, but I said, 'Because I must go soon. I must sleep. I'm very tired.'

'Tired.'

'Yes. Maria, why didn't you tell me he was here?'

'Who was here?'

'Laurence. My friend. He said he's come to the village here, behind the shop. A few times. Why didn't you tell me?'

But she shook her head, and her frowning face was blank. No, she said, she hadn't seen him. She didn't know what I meant.

Was she lying? I looked hard at her to see. Then I noticed for the first time that she wasn't happy.

'What's the matter?' I said.

No, nothing was the matter.

A moment later a tear went down her cheek. I got up and went to her, but she turned away from me.

'What's this? Maria, what's this?'

There was a bruise, a darkening down one side of her face. And I saw that she'd been hiding it, sitting away from the light, angled away from me.

No, she said, it was nothing.

'What do you mean, nothing? How can it be nothing? Where does it come from?'

'No, no.' She waved it away; another tear fell. Suddenly I understood all the questions that she'd asked when I arrived. *You don't come. Why, why?* I tried to put my arm around her, but she got up and started rearranging the wooden animals on the shelves. After a minute or two she said, 'You go now.'

'I want to stay.'

'No. Now is danger. Problem, problem.'

'Can I come back later?'

She shook her head. 'Is better you go. Tomorrow you come.'

I stood up, dusting off my knees, feeling awkward and ashamed. Because I didn't know what else to do, I fished in my pocket for money. I held it out to her: fifty rand. But tonight, for the first time, she didn't want it; she seemed almost not to see it; she shook her head again. It was something else she wanted.

'You come tomorrow night?'

'Yes.'

'You promise tomorrow?'

'Yes,' I said, and I meant it with my whole heart, but she looked at me as if I was lying.

On Monday mornings there was a staff meeting in the office. In theory this was when patients were discussed, particular cases focused on with a view to improving our work, any problems or ideas aired and shared. In practice it was an exercise carried out mostly on paper: roll-call was taken, Dr Ngema said a few words, everybody went away again.

But this morning Dr Ngema said, 'There is a . . . special announcement today.'

We were all looking at her. She shifted uncomfortably and gestured to Laurence.

He looked important. He had dressed in his smartest clothes and combed and re-combed his hair so that the wet strands gleamed separately. His white coat was buttoned stiffly, all the way to the chin. He stood up, a sheaf of papers in his hand.

'Um. Yes. Thank you. I just want to say that on Thursday . . . this Thursday morning . . . I will be running a clinic in one of the villages near by.'

A faint consternation went through the room. There was a shifting of chairs, a sound of papers being rustled.

'Excuse me?' Claudia said.

'A clinic. We will be running a clinic'

Jorge coughed. 'I don't understand. You want . . . ?'

Into the silence a first trace of dismay was creeping. Laurence's face had fallen slightly and he looked at the papers in his hand as if the answer was written there.

Dr Ngema coughed; we turned to her pinched face. 'This is an idea,' she said, 'an idea put forward by Laurence. It's a . . . very good idea, I think. But it's entirely voluntary, of course. If any of you want to go and help out, it would be very much . . .'

'Appreciated,' Laurence said. He was still standing.

'I myself won't be able to go,' Dr Ngema said. 'Prior work commitments.'

'Maybe I should explain,' Laurence said. 'The plan is for me to do a presentation. I'm not a hundred per cent sure yet, there are so many things . . . but I was thinking, a talk on sanitation and hygiene, you know, then a talk on HIV-Aids. Then there'll be condom distribution, it's about all we have to distribute at this stage, but more stuff will come, I'm sure. Um, then there'll be the part where people line up to see one of us, for whatever problem they have. That's all I can think of. Oh, it's happening at a village near by, I've forgotten its name, but I did write it down somewhere . . .'

An astounded pause followed on.

'Excuse please,' Claudia said, 'but why is this for, why?'

Laurence said, 'I thought it would be a way of drawing attention to the hospital, of making people aware that we're here. And of actually doing something.'

That was not a good word to use; the next silence was very cold. When he sat down the energy in the room had gone flat.

I waited a few seconds before I raised my hand and said, 'I support this idea, this initiative, of Laurence's, completely. But I'm afraid it won't be possible for me to attend.'

I could feel Laurence staring at me.

'Why is that, Frank?' Dr Ngema said.

'I have to go away for a few days. Personal reasons.'

'I'm not aware of any . . .'

'It's just come up,' I said. 'I was going to discuss it with you later.'

There was an overwhelming inertia in the room as the meeting broke up. I went out quickly, but Laurence caught up with me as I was crossing the open plot of ground on my way back to the room. 'Why, Frank, why?'

'Oh, they'll be more enthusiastic on the day, Laurence, don't worry about them.'

'I don't mean that. I know they don't like my plan, I don't care about them. It's you, Frank. Why won't you be there?'

'I have to go to Pretoria. I can't help it, Laurence. Bad timing. It's my divorce agreement. Has to be done.'

'Oh.' His face fell. Divorce, signing: adult affairs—a world he didn't know. 'But it's such a pity. It was your idea, Frank.'

'It wasn't my idea,' I said, surprised at the vehemence in my voice. 'This was your idea entirely.'

'But to go to that particular village . . .'

'It wasn't an idea, Laurence. It wasn't even a suggestion. I was just talking without thinking.'

'Oh,' he said, 'oh,' and he trailed the rest of the way behind me without speaking, his head down.

I went to see Dr Ngema that afternoon. She was in her office with the door open, writing at her desk. When she saw me she closed the door and sat us both down on the low chairs, face to face, as she always did for personal conversations.

There was nothing she could say; today my haggard, troubled face gave me a kind of power. 'Of course,' she said. 'I'll arrange the schedule, Frank. Don't worry about it.' It was the first time I'd asked for leave in three years. She put a hand to my shoulder, then let it drop. Trying to show sympathy for a pain I didn't feel; my marriage had effectively ended years ago. 'Take off from tomorrow, if you like. I'll see to it.'

'Thank you, I appreciate that.'

'There is something else . . .'

I'd been waiting for this; I remembered her cryptic allusions at the party.

'It's related to the clinic. Indirectly. Actually, it's about the job.'

'The job?'

'This job. My job.' She leaned forward. 'Your job. Things are moving again, Frank.'

'Are they?' I'd had this same conversation with her so many times by now that I could only give a tired imitation of enthusiasm. 'That's good.'

'I think it's really going to happen this time. I can't give you the details, but it's very promising.'

'That's good news, Ruth. I'm very pleased to hear it.'

'Which is why I'm not so sure this clinic is such a good idea. I know you support it, Frank. You've helped Laurence along. For the best reasons, of course, I don't doubt that. But we don't need any big new initiatives right now.'

'Oh. Yes. I see.'

'I support change and innovation,' she said plaintively. 'You know that. But we don't want to rock the boat. Not at this point.'

'I understand.'

'Thank you, Frank. You've always been very . . . understanding. And you know when you're the big boss here you can do whatever you want. You can change the world!'

I nodded carefully. She was being careful, too, in the way she spoke to me, but now some of her real feeling showed through.

'I like Laurence. He means well, I can see that. But sometimes he . . .'

'I understand.'

'Yes. The way he talked just now, for example. "It's a way of actually doing something." Does he mean we're not doing anything here?'

'He's young. He speaks without thinking.'

'You're loyal. He's your friend. That's good. But he's . . . he's arrogant sometimes. Too big for his boots.'

I nodded again and her face closed over; the irritation and dislike were gone. Or hidden. She said: 'I don't mean anything bad. You know that. I just think he would've been happier at another hospital.'

'You may be right.'

'I like him. Don't get me wrong.'

'I understand.'

'Thank you for understanding, Frank.'

When I got back to the room, Laurence was dressing for duty.

'I've been thinking about it,' he said defiantly, 'and I don't care.'

'About what?'

'If they don't want to do the clinic, I'll just go ahead on my own. I don't care. They don't matter. I just wish you were going to be there, Frank. That's the only thing that bothers me.'

'Next time, maybe.'

He shot me a look of such injured gratitude that I felt a pang of sympathy for him. He was alone, and he didn't know it. And the quality I'd seen in his face that first day was back again, flickering visibly beneath the skin, almost nameable for a second.

When he was gone I walked around aimlessly, straightening the furniture, wiping toothpaste off the mirror, dusting the windowsill, and somewhere in the middle of my vindictive housekeeping I found Tehogo's cassettes in a heap on the floor. I stacked them up neatly, ready for him to collect; but when everything was clean I took them down the passage myself.

Was I looking for something? I had no motive in my head, but the moment I was outside the door I was conscious of something heightened and alert in me. Something watchful.

It was the last door in the passage. The light outside had broken a long time ago and of course nobody had fixed it. Even now, late in the day, I was standing in the dark when I knocked. He didn't answer. He was asleep, I thought, and I knocked harder and the door shifted under my hand.

It wasn't locked. Through the small crack I could see the edge of an unmade bed and a table with ashtrays and orange peel on it. I put out my hand and with the very rips of my fingers I pushed gently on the door—as if it wasn't me, as if the wind was doing it. The door swung further open. I put my head through and called his name. But the bed was empty and he didn't come out of the bathroom.

The place was filthy. The floor was strewn with litter—old cigarette boxes, empty bottles, used glasses. The sheets on the bed looked foul. There were magazines lying everywhere and a stale fug of smoke and sweat and tiredness hung in the air.

I called his name again as I went in, but I knew he wasn't there: it was like a spell to carry me over the threshold. And at that moment the afternoon outside, and my reason for being there, fell away; I was entering into a place inside myself, a sordid little room of my own heart, where a secret was stored.

But of course this was Tehogo's room—and I saw that too. Maybe it was even, in some peculiar way and in spite of his absence, the first time I had ever seen Tehogo. He was an enigmatic presence in the hospital, surly, opaque, with more attitude than personality . . . but my eye fell now on traces of a hidden nature. All the magazines lying around were women's magazines, full of fashion and glamour, and he'd cut out pictures from them and stuck them on the walls. Sunsets and beaches and improbable airbrushed landscapes. Women posing in underwear or fancy outfits. The images gave off a longing and sentiment and pathos. And next to the bed, in a little cleared space on top of a table, was a framed photograph of an elderly couple. They were obviously dressed up for the picture, stiff and awkward in formal clothes, standing slightly apart and rigid outside a house somewhere. His parents? Impossible to know, but it was the one item in the chaos that he'd tried to give a certain value.

My eye went further, looking, looking. And I was so tangled up in all the angles and edges of the discarded junk that it took me a good few minutes to see. But when I did see, all the other stuff became extraneous, a distracting trapping piled around the truth. The truth was in the myriad little bits of metal, the taps and pipes and bed-frames, casually stacked or piled or leaning against each other. The whole room was full of it. And then I knew.

I went quietly back out of the room without leaving the cassettes and closed the door behind me. When I passed Tehogo in the passage in the main building a little while later, whistling to himself as he pushed a trolley along, I nodded to him and said hellos.

11

Dr Ngema changed the schedule. But I didn't go away on Tuesday. I had things on my mind, things to brood over. On Tuesday night Laurence and I were in the recreation room, watching the television, both of us wrapped up in private thoughts, until I suggested we go down to Mama's place for a drink.

'I don't think so, Frank. Not tonight. I'm not in the mood.'

'Come on, it's on me. There's something I need to talk about.'

He perked up a bit at this. Gossip and intrigue; something to take him out of himself. And when we were down at Mama's, the mood and energy lifted us both. It was hard to believe that this little courtyard—so brightly lit, so full of people—was in the middle of so much desolation and emptiness. You stepped out of gloom into warmth, talk, loud music.

'What's going on here?' Laurence said. 'Is it a party?'

'There've been some changes since you were here.'

He'd heard about the soldiers. But he'd never seen them, or thought anything might be different because of them. But even I was amazed at what had happened: there were at least twice as many people as before, twice as much noise. Something really did seem to have changed.

'I'm going to get a pool table soon,' Mama told us happily as she had two extra chairs brought in for us. 'Business is good.'

I felt eyes on me and saw Colonel Moller in a corner of the courtyard, alone at a table, with a glass in front of him.

'Are they really doing something, these soldiers? Or are they just sitting here drinking?'

She pretended to look shocked. 'They are working very hard. Every day they are going out to look for people.'

'But do they ever catch anybody?'

'I don't know about that,' she said, with a shrug and a smile. That part of their presence had nothing to do with her. She brought our drinks and went away again, into the loud, busy crowd.

'What did you want to talk about, Frank? Is it the clinic?'

'Oh, no, no. Nothing to do with that. I have an ethical dilemma.'

'Really? Tell me about it.'

So I told him—flatly, without colour—about going into Tehogo's room, about what I saw there. When I'd finished, his face didn't change. Then it did. It took a moment for comprehension to break through, like a finger rummaging through his ordered version of the world.

'You mean . . . ?'

I nodded heavily.

'He's been stealing . . . ? Been taking . . . ? He's the one?'

'Well, it looks that way, doesn't it? Maybe there's another explanation, of course . . .'

'What other explanation?'

I shrugged.

'There isn't one. There's no other explanation. Oh, wow, Frank, I can't believe this.' He'd actually gone pale. His expression had the shock of somebody forced to look directly at something he'd been trying to pretend wasn't there. Then it cleared. 'But what's your dilemma?'

'Well, obviously . . . I don't know what to do now.'

'Don't know what to do? But you must tell Dr Ngema.'

'It's not as simple as that, Laurence. There are issues to be considered.'

'Like what?'

'Like Tehogo's background. He's had a rough time. It doesn't feel right just to—'

'But he's stealing.'

'Yes.'

'That's the only issue, Frank. You can't think about anything else.'

So simple: one issue, all the complexities and contradictions reduced to a single moral needle-point. And that was Laurence. Something was either good or bad, clearly and definingly so, and you acted accordingly.

'I don't think it's that easy,' I said with sad satisfaction.

'Why not?' The shock was back in his face now, tinged with dismay; he was balanced on a brink, dark gravity pulling at him.

'Let's leave it. We don't see things the same way.'

'But I'm trying to understand, Frank. Tell me!'

'I don't know how to explain.'

'You're too good, Frank. You have too much sympathy.'

'Anyway, it's my problem.'

But I could see—though we didn't talk any more about it then— that I had handed the problem on to him. He looked troubled and preoccupied for the rest of the evening, while some of the noise and ribaldry of the place rubbed off on me. I had a good time.

It was the next day, while he watched me throw some clothes into a suitcase, that he brought it up again. 'Have you decided,' he asked tentatively, 'have you worked out . . . what to do?'

'Nothing.'

'But you'd better do something soon, or it'll be too late.'

'Better that way.'

He looked pained. 'It'll just go on. He'll just carry on taking and stealing . . .'

I sat down, smiling. 'Do you really care about it so much? It's just an abandoned building, when you come down to it.'

'No! I mean, yes—I do care about it.'

'I think, in this case, human feelings are more important.'

After a pause he said awkwardly, 'You know, I could do it if you like.'

'Do what?'

'Report . . . what happened.'

'But you didn't see it.'

'Yes, I know that, but . . . somebody has to do something. And if it's too difficult for you . . . I just thought that . . .'

He squirmed, the ethical dilemma all his now, while I looked down on his battle in the real world. I said, 'I don't know about that. It doesn't seem right.'

'It's just a thought, Frank. I wouldn't use your name at all.'

'Well,' I said, 'you must follow your conscience, Laurence. Whatever you think is best.'

We didn't talk more about it, but he seemed suddenly relieved. And so was I. The future was taking shape, untainted by my hands; and an unwitting complicity had drawn us closer.

He said, 'Do you have time for some table tennis before you go?'

'Um. Yes, okay. I'm only leaving tonight anyway, I prefer to drive in the dark.'

And over in the recreation room, while we jumped around in the sun, knocking the ball back and forth to each other, it was almost the way it had used to be—companionable and friendly, a happy connection. Later we got tired. He threw the bat down and collapsed on to the couch, pushing a long strand of hair out of his eyes.

'I got a letter from Zanele,' he announced.

'That's good.'

'She's split up with me. She says it's over.'

'But I thought you two had such plans and schemes.'

'So did I.'

'What did she say?'

For the first time today a real feeling touched his face: a distant pain, like a subterranean tremor. 'Oh, you know. It's false . . . the whole thing wasn't working . . . too long apart, no connection any more.' His expression closed over again. 'The usual story. Blah blah.'

Now it came: the guilt, spreading in me like a stain. I avoided his eyes. 'I'm sorry, Laurence.'

'That's okay.' He shrugged. 'The funny thing is, I don't care too much. You think you love something so badly, but when it's gone you find out you don't care so much.'

'Sometimes that's true.'

'Work,' he said. 'Work is the only thing that matters.'

He really meant it. I stood looking down at him on the couch, considering this. He was almost sexless; his only real passion was in work. But work had never carried that sort of meaning for me; it was just one more version of futile activity, going nowhere.

He said abruptly, 'I suppose you're thinking about your wife.'

I was completely startled by this; I wasn't thinking about her at all.

'What does it feel like to be married?'

I didn't know how to answer, but I had a memory of the first night after the wedding. We'd gone away into the country for a honeymoon. The woman who had somehow transformed into the other half of my life was in the bathroom and suddenly the whole world outside the room also seemed strange, unknown, maybe dangerous. I had a sensation of panic that was indistinguishable from happiness. The feeling was intense, but it passed quickly.

I said, 'I don't want to talk about that.'

When I started on the long drive that night, I saw three things close to the town that became connected in my mind. The first came on the little stretch of tributary road, before I reached the main road. Whenever I got to the bend from where the old army encampment was visible I always slowed down; usually there was nothing to see, just blackness and bush, but tonight there was a light burning. It could have been a fire or a lamp: a tiny spark almost buried in the dark. Then it went out, or I was past. That got me thinking. I'd been bothered by something the Brigadier had said to Zanele, that night in the garden: *It is hard. Very hard. One day to be living here. Next day living in a tent.* The point about a tent, of course, is that it can be uprooted and moved; he could have meant anywhere. But the old army camp still had its old tents, at least two or three of them, and it was the place, after all, from which he'd come. His ghost had always felt thicker there, more substantial; and now I wondered.

I remembered the two men working in the garden, and the brown military overalls they were wearing, and I was still thinking about them when more army uniforms showed up in the head-lamps. New uniforms, the new army; but for a moment it was like the old days again, with soldiers looming in the night, guns in their hands. A line of lights on the road, metal barriers dragged across the tar, a torch drawing me over to the side. A roadblock. But this was Colonel Moller and his men, doing a different sort of work. I recognized the upright bodies I'd seen strung along the line of the bar, but tonight they were searching through car boots and cubby-holes, covering each other with rifles. The black man who questioned me was brisk and polite. Where are you coming from? Where are you going? Would you open up the back, please, I want to take a look.

As I pulled away again I looked for Colonel Moller. I couldn't see him, but I could feel him near by somewhere, another kind of ghost, one that stayed with me through all the bends and dips in the road until I got to Maria's shack.

And then it happened. The third thing. I hadn't gone back to visit Maria on the night I promised I would, or on the night that followed. I'd been too preoccupied with what was going on at the hospital—Tehogo and the stealing—and I knew the shack would still be there, whenever I was ready to go. I had it in mind to stop there tonight on my way, but I saw now that the white car was parked outside.

And that was it: the white car. An arbitrary image, one I carried around unthinkingly in me, but now I remembered, with an inner flash like lightning, the white car parked outside the Brigadier's house on the hill. And though I didn't even know whether that other car resembled this one, I became instantly certain that they were the same.

Instantly certain—and then uncertain again . . . but the connection was made. And the sense that I had, as I drove on and on through the dark, a sense that was like a huge disquiet powering me along, was of the interlocking pieces of a puzzle just beyond my grasp, eluding me.

I drove with the window down, letting the hot wind go through the car. The escarpment rose and lifted me, and soon I was clear of the forest and in the open grass land of the veld. The night was very big here, spread like a huge canvas on the taut wires of the horizon. The car rose and fell on dark undulations, the light from the headlamps tiny and lost. There was comfort in being so small. At one place there was a veld fire burning. I could see the flames from a long way off and, as I got closer, a congregation of cars and people. The flames were very big and bright and black smoke boiled and rolled in the artificial yellow light. I slowed, but I was waved past and the heat of the fire beat on my face as the weird midnight coven sank away in the mirror.

Then the little towns, shuttered, sleeping, barred. Other roads joined this one, feeding it, fattening it up. Pylons and smokestacks against the sky. Garages lit in neon with shivering attendants sleeping in booths. Far off in the distance, cities burned like smouldering piles of coal. All the elements of a foreign world were coming together for me, assembling to make a picture of the past.

I arrived as dawn was breaking. But I didn't go straight to the house. I drove aimlessly for a while through the suburban streets, feeling the presence of people in the houses, behind the walls, in the gardens. Even the first stirrings of activity—a few cars, a couple of workers on the pavements—made the place seem unnaturally full to me.

My father lived out in the southern part of the city, in a rich, exclusive suburb. Broad tree-lined streets, a sense of distance and light. It was the house I'd grown up in from my early teenage years, though the bottom half of the garden had since been divided off and sold. Another change was the wall that had sprung up around the property. In my day there had been only a fence. Now the wall just seemed to climb and climb.

My stepmother answered the intercom when I buzzed. 'This is Frank junior,' I told her, and the gate swung heavily open for me on its big hinges. I parked outside the garage at the top of the driveway. Plants grew green and heavy under looming trees, the brick castle leaned overhead.

She came out to meet me, dressed in smartly casual clothes, face heavily made up. But all the makeup couldn't conceal a little pained place in her expression. Valerie was my father's fourth wife, but she was in fact a few years younger than me. We had never found a comfortable level at which to speak to each other.

She kissed me awkwardly on the cheek. 'Dad's in the bath. How was the drive? Do you need help with your bag? You must be tired.' Her anxiety buoyed me up the stairs, into the house. Two maids danced and grovelled in blue uniforms with frilly aprons, both of them barefoot so as not to spoil the carpets. Of which there were many, oriental with cryptic designs; they were a passion of my father's.

'Let me see you. Oh, you look more and more like Dad.' I wished she wouldn't call him that, as if he was father to both of us; she was too much like a sister already, with her small, painted, worried face hiding secret rivalry with me. 'You can have your old room, Frank. I've kept it just the way it was.'

Each of my father's wives had insisted on redoing the house—a way, maybe, of staking a claim when they sensed that their stay was temporary. Since I'd left home my room had been changed and repainted a few times, so Valerie's idea of preserving my little childhood refuge was to hang my old model airplanes from the ceiling and to set up some embarrassing photographs from my schooldays on the windowsill. Frank in the fifth rugby team. Frank as deputy head boy, shaking the hand of the headmaster. Otherwise the room was as pretty and clinical as a mid-range hotel, full of fabrics and colours my mother would never have contemplated.

'Do you want to shower after the long drive? You must be tired, do you want to sleep? Do you want some breakfast?'

I sat out on the back patio, drinking black coffee. I could hear my father in the bathroom, splashing and humming to himself. Once he burped. He sounded in a good mood. Valerie came out and made a pretence of fiddling with the pot plants on the stairs, then called out instructions to a gardener hidden somewhere in the foliage outside. She went back in and busied herself until she could hear my father was on his way, then came out with her own coffee and sat herself near by.

'How long are you down for, Frank?'

'Just a day or two. I'm here to see Karen.'

'Karen? Oh, that's nice.' Her voice had a hopeful upward note.

'No, no.' But before I could explain, my father came out on to the patio.

Frank Eloff senior was in his middle sixties by now, but he had the body and voice of someone fifteen years younger. A big, loose, long frame, a handsome face that was always, however faintly, smiling. He was groomed and clipped and elegant—even now, first thing in the morning, shaved and scented, in his paisley dressing gown and Turkish slippers. He shook hands with me, his customary greeting or farewell even when I was a boy, and his hand carried some of the damp warmth of the bathroom, or maybe his hair oil.

'Frank!'

'Dad.'

'It's an unusual surprise. To see you, I mean. I hope you're taking a proper holiday for a change.'

'No, this isn't a holiday, Dad. I have some personal business to attend to.'

'Personal business.'

'He's here to see Karen,' Valerie said primly.

'Oh, yes?'

'It's to sign the divorce papers, actually,' I said, and there was a noticeable lowering of pressure on the patio. My father was of the opinion that my separation from Karen was responsible for the decline of my career, and he frequently expressed the hope that we'd get back together again.

I heard Valerie say, 'Oh.'

'Well, Frank, I'm sorry to hear that.' My father put on his sombre look, which didn't quite erase his smile, and made his voice low. 'Is that final? Whose decision is that? Wouldn't it be better to wait a little longer?'

'Her decision. It's final, yes. They're getting married and moving to Australia.'

'Oh. Well. Yes. A lot of the young people are moving away. Very sad.'

'I'd move,' Valerie announced. 'I'd move tomorrow. But your dad won't have it.'

'Still the best country in the world,' my father said, grinning. 'Still the best quality of life. Now I have to get dressed.'

The morning sun was hot on the patio, so while my father dressed we moved inside to the study. This was the biggest room in the house, lined with books and the prominently displayed accolades of my father's career. The strongest memory of my adolescent years— which seemed to be one memory but was really many, overlaid on each other—was of facing him across his desk, with that clutter of photographs and publicity like a cloud suspended behind him.

I went up close to look at them now. Most of the pictures showed Frank senior in his early forties, with his broad gleaming grin and backswept hair. In some he was posing with actors and politicians from twenty years ago. I was surprised to see a couple of newer photographs among them; he still wasn't forgotten.

My father had been something of a smash hit in his time. An unusual fate for a doctor. But he'd seized his moment when it came. He'd started out as a small-town boy from a poor family, who'd gone to medical school on a scholarship from a mining company. After he qualified he went to work for this same company as a doctor on one of their mines. Bad beginnings: but everything turned around for him when there was a terrible accident underground one day and he was on the scene. For one straight forty-eight-hour period, my father crouched in a crumbling tunnel, setting bones, performing amputations, stitching up wounds. He saved the lives of six or seven miners who would almost certainly have died.

The achievement was real. But it's hard, a quarter of a century later, not to see it through cynical eyes. This was back in the time when the big white dream was turning grey; they needed a poster boy to make them look good, and for a while Frank senior was it. He did look good. He had the dash of a matinee idol, with his boyish forelock and toothy grin. And the media jumped on him. There were front-page articles in the national papers, interviews on the radio, magazine features on his difficult struggle to success. Never mind the miners, who went back to their underground obscurity; my father was the hero of the day.

It all might still have faded again, as quickly as it began, if it hadn't been for television. TV had just started in South Africa and, after an appearance on the news, somebody decided that my father would be ideal as the host on a new programme. It was a medical quiz show, featuring Frank senior as the suave quiz-master, asking questions of various local personalities. The public loved it, and him. The media attention went on and on. Piles of fan mail arrived at the house. Somewhere in the middle of all this my mother died, but I truly think he hardly noticed—though he did get some more press coverage out of it.

He somehow managed, through all of this clamour and glamour, to keep a serious career going too. Not at the mine any more:

he'd moved on from there. But by all accounts he was a gifted surgeon and much in demand. Of course the publicity couldn't have hurt much either. He'd also branched out into marketing his own products—hair straightener and skin lightener for black people, all kinds of cosmetic creams for white women. These things were still on the shelves, still bringing in money for him.

It was a spectacular, unlikely rise to stardom, and it hadn't quite faded yet. He was still fêted and dined and dandled, wheeled out for special events, giving honorary lectures and appearing on panels. It was a circus. Nobody cared that the one singular achievement of my father's life was five, ten, thirty years ago and that he'd never done a substantial thing since. No, he would be young and brilliant for ever.

So there was pressure on me. I had something to prove. I imagined not only that I wanted to be like him, but that it would be easy to do. But of course it hadn't happened like that, and now the pictures and words on the wall were like a judgement on me.

I heard him coming and went to sit down. He'd changed into golf clothes, slacks and a short-sleeved shirt. 'I hope you don't mind, Frank, it's a game I arranged before I knew you were coming.'

'No problem, I'm going to see Karen this morning anyway.'

'What is this all about anyway, this thing with Karen?' He settled himself seriously behind the desk. 'Do you want me to have a word with Sam?'

Sam was Karen's father, an old friend of my father's.

'What? No, no. That wouldn't change anything.'

'Are you sure? A bit of discreet pressure—'

'I'll leave you two to talk,' Valerie said.

'No, don't. It's not for discussion.' I sounded very firm. The last thing I wanted: my father having a quiet word, as though the whole matter could be settled by him. But he didn't like to be spoken to this way. He said angrily to Valerie, 'Those flowers are dead.'

He was referring to a big bouquet on the mantelpiece, which was turning brown.

'I've told Betty to take them.'

'Well, tell her again. I don't like them there.' This was the other side of his expansive charm, a mood of petulant fury that was also centred entirely on himself.

I got up. 'I'm going to shower and change. I'll see you both later.'

'I'm not trying to interfere, Frank. You know that.'

'Of course I know that, Dad.'

I went to my room and showered and shaved and dressed myself in clean clothes. All the time the noises from the big space of the house radiated in: the throb of the washing machine, the hum of air-conditioners, the almost-noiseless flurry of servants cleaning. All strange sounds to me, remembered from long ago. And the face that looked back at me from the bathroom mirror was the same combination of memory and strangeness. If you looked hard you could just make out the schoolboy from the photographs on the windowsill. But he was very different now. The rosy flush had gone, the hair was darker and thinner, the flesh on the cheeks and throat had thickened. It was a face in slow decay, tumbling and sliding down from its bones, sprouting veins and moles and blemishes. You could see an old man in it already, and the expression on his face had a quality of defeat.

Karen and Mike lived in a large penthouse apartment in an area of the city that was almost entirely flat-land. A middle-class area, not very rich. But Sam, Karen's father, owned the whole block, as well as a number of other blocks near by. That is not to mention his other properties around the country. He'd given the penthouse to Karen as a wedding present when she married me.

Sam had known my father since the early days, when they'd both been at university together. My father was fond of telling me how he and Sam had been close long before money had entered the scene for either of them. In those days Sam was just a hopeful studying law, my father still the poor country mouse trying to shape his future. The moral, I suppose, was that their friendship was based on real values of liking and respect, not the transitory shifting sands of fame and income.

Sam didn't like me. He never had. Maybe he saw what neither I nor my father was willing to acknowledge: that my future wasn't glorious, that I wasn't made of the same fine stuff as Frank Eloff senior. Nevertheless, he was gracious when his youngest daughter and I fell in love. I'd known and hung around with Karen from my earliest years. There was something inevitable, in a social sense, about our coming together. Similar backgrounds of privilege and wealth, similar families forged almost single-handedly by the efforts of determined men with low beginnings. It didn't matter that neither Karen nor I had exceptional qualities. Our lives could be made exceptional by money.

Karen was a bit aimless, a bit of a drifter. She started studying one thing, then dropped it and moved on to something else. She finally completed a degree in drama, which she claimed to feel passionate about, but after a few thankless walk-ons she dropped that too. At the time that I married her, just after my two years in the army, she had gone into a business with her mother, running a couple of gift shops that did quite well, but after a while she got bored. It was in the empty period that followed, when she was playing at being an idle madam at home, that her affair with Mike started; for a time I tormented myself with the idea that if she'd only been working . . .

These days she called herself an interior designer. And I must admit she had an eye. She'd redone the whole penthouse, transforming it from an expensive mausoleum to something airy and comfortable, if a little upmarket for my sensibilities. Lots of open space, wooden floors, tall windows looking out on the city.

Karen's mother, Jacqui, was just leaving as I arrived. She was walking carefully in high heels, as if to keep the tall pillar of hair balanced on her head. Old and immaculate, mummified under makeup that threatened to crack with even her driest smile, she offered one cheek without a change in expression. 'Frank,' she murmured. 'I know you have an appointment, I'm on my way out.'

'I thought you and Sam were in France.' They'd emigrated six years ago.

'Back for business. The third time this year. You know Sam, he never lets go.'

'No.'

'And you, Frank. Still working so hard?'

'Um. Yes. As hard as ever.'

'I hear you do such wonderful work up there. Amongst the rural blacks.'

Karen only greeted me when her mother had gone. She pressed her lips to my cheek, a quick dry peck, and there was the momentary feeling of her bony hips in my hands.

'You've lost weight,' I told her.

'You've put some on. You look terrible, Frank. What's happened to you?'

'Nothing. Same old life.'

'Let's go through to the lounge.'

Once we had settled ourselves on the big leather armchairs, above the city skyline, she picked up a sheaf of papers from the coffee table. 'Here. Business first. I have it all ready.'

'So I see.'

'I'm sure you'll want to have your lawyer look it over.'

'No,' I said. 'I'll sign it now. Give me a pen.'

She was astonished. 'Don't you even want to read it through yourself?'

I tried to, but even from the first line—*the marriage of Karen and Frank has broken down irretrievably*—my eyes slid off the words. It had all been talked about so endlessly, and none of it had anything to do with the way my life was now.

'Is there anything in here I should know about?'

'Meaning what? That I would cheat you? I wouldn't cheat you, Frank. What a horrible suggestion. It's all just confirming the arrangement we have now. What's mine is mine, what's yours is yours. What do you have, for God's sake, that you think I would want?'

'Just checking.' I took the gleaming fountain-pen she had set down on the table and signed the last page. The scratching of the nib made an almost inaudible rustle that maybe only my ears were tuned to: the sound of eleven years collapsing.

'There,' she said. She turned each page for me to sign. Then she took the document and the pen and carried the whole lot through to the bedroom, out of reach, as if I might change my mind. When she came back in she was more at ease with me.

'You shouldn't just sign things without checking, Frank. It's typical of you, not to care. You never know what could happen.'

'It's typical of you to get irritated that I might think you were cheating me, and then irritated because I didn't check that you aren't.'

She smiled as if I'd complimented her. 'Well, it's done. The court thing is just a formality. I'll let you know when it's over. Do you want something to drink?'

'No, thanks. I've had some coffee already.'

'I always drink juice in the morning. I'm going to give you some juice, Frank. It might improve that colouring of yours.'

There were maids flitting through the background here too, but Karen went to the kitchen herself and came back with two tall glasses of orange juice. She sat in a different chair now, closer to me, and I realized we were going to have a personal chat.

'Frank. I want to ask you something. Bluntly.'

'Go ahead.'

'How do you feel towards Mike? I mean, these days, now that the dust has settled.'

'How do I feel towards him? I think he's a snake who stole my wife from me.'

'Oh, Frank. Come on. It's been years. Can't we move on?'

'I have moved on. But I haven't forgiven him.'

It was odd how clear this was to me: even though my love for Karen had dwindled to a faint interior glow, my hatred for Mike still burned big and bright. Past a certain point, maybe, a person's character defines itself and stays fixed in your mind. I could see Mike's picture on the wall, a recent one, and even though the balding, corpulent figure hardly resembled the young man I'd been friends with, something in him—or in me, perhaps—felt constant, unchanging, immovable.

'That's such a pity, Frank. It's such a pity you're so . . . vengeful. Mike wants to get past it. He wants to . . . I don't know, purge himself before we go. He's told me, actually, that he misses you sometimes.'

'Has he?'

'Oh, why do I bother? I thought that maybe now the divorce is all signed and official . . . but I can see it's a waste of time. Why are you so bitter, Frank? Is it from being stuck up there in the *bundu* for so long? Don't you think it's time to come back to civilization?'

'No.'

'Do you think we feel sorry for you? Mike says you like to suffer to get attention.'

'I don't care what Mike says.'

'Well, it's a pity. That's all I can say. He likes you, actually.'

'Listen,' I said. 'You may not believe it, but I want to be there. In my own way I'm nearly happy.'

She studied me for a bit, then leaned towards me, and I could see she was going to be daring.

'Do you have . . . somebody . . . up there . . . ?'

'Yes,' I said, startling myself with the certainty of my reply. And it was startling, too, how readily the image of Maria came to mind. Alone and waiting in the rough wooden shack. For me.

Karen nodded, smiling tightly. 'Who is she? One of the other doctors, I suppose.'

'No. Somebody else. From outside the hospital.'

'Well, I can hear you aren't going to tell me more. But it would be nice, Frank, if we could get together. Me and Mike and you and your lady friend. We could go out for dinner or something. Think about it.'

I almost laughed. It was absurd to think of Maria amongst these people—even among this furniture. And I saw how far I had moved from the normal way of things.

I drank the orange juice and set the glass down. 'I'd better get going.'

'All right. I suppose you've got to do the family thing. I was sorry to hear about your father.'

'What?'

This had dropped so casually into the conversation that I almost didn't catch it.

She looked taken aback. 'Well, I . . . I heard he was ill.'

'Not as far as I know.'

'I don't know, Frank. I'm sorry, forget about it, I never spoke.'

But I kept thinking on the drive back and when I got to the house I called Karen again. She was speaking in a brisk, defensive voice again; our intimate moment was over.

'I really want to know,' I said. 'Whatever it is, I wish you'd tell me.'

'I don't know anything, Frank. I got confused with something else I heard.'

'I don't believe you.'

'Don't believe me then. But I wouldn't lie to you.'

I spent the rest of the day at the house, wandering in the long passages and the narrow paths of the garden. My stepmother hovered anxiously, between repeated expeditions to the shops, the hairdresser, the garage, and once or twice I almost brought myself to ask her: *is he ill*? But the question was too big and brash for all the fake gentility around us. It would have seemed rude.

It was evening when my father got back from the club. He said he'd played badly. He'd had a few drinks and seemed irritable, but he didn't look sick to me. His voice was still loud and sure of itself, expressing opinions like truths, making jokes, and it was only when we came to dessert that he remembered I wasn't there on holiday.

'Oh, Frank. I meant to ask you. It just went out of my mind. How did it go, your talk with Karen?'

'All right. It's signed and done.'

'What? The papers? Finished?'

'Yes.'

'But I . . . I thought it was just a talk. Was it wise to rush through things like that?'

'It's been a few years, Dad. No rush involved.'

'I'm sorry, Frank, that it's ended up like this.'

'It was pretty inevitable, Dad.'

'Yes. Still. I wish you'd let me try to work something out with Sam.'

'It would've made no difference.'

'Maybe. Maybe.' He fiddled with his napkin. 'Are you going to stay with us for a few days more?'

'Afraid not. I have to go back in the morning.'

'So soon?' Valerie put on her sad face. 'You only just arrived.'

'I know. But I had to get special permission to come. They need me up there.' And though none of it was true, and I had only just decided to leave, I knew I didn't belong here. My place was somewhere else, in the rural hospital room full of cheap government furniture, where none of my father's certainties applied.

'They need you?' His tone was scoffing. 'Are you still taking orders from that black woman? Isn't this the time, Frank, to think about moving back here?'

'I think I'm on the verge of something up there.'

'The verge of what?'

'Promotion. It looks as if I may become head of the hospital soon.'

'But we've been hearing this story for years already. You were supposed to be the big boss when you went up there in the first place.'

'I know that. But it's all shifting around. It really is going to happen now.'

'I could speak to people down here, Frank. We could get you a post in one of the local hospitals. Nothing special, but with better prospects than you have right now.'

'My prospects are fine.' Indignation rose in me, and I found myself describing, in self-righteous tones, what my future was going to be: Dr Ngema would leave, I would step into her shoes, I would make things happen, in a few years I too would be eligible for another post somewhere . . . As I sketched out this sequence of events, it seemed virtually certain that everything would happen just as I'd described it. And the hospital—which my father had never once visited—became like a place I'd never seen either: a necessary place, full of patients and work and selflessness, where adversity and sacrifice were joined.

'Well, I don't know about any of that.' He pushed his pudding away, half-eaten. 'This country has changed so much I don't recognize it any more. All I know is, I couldn't do it. I wouldn't mind working under a black, but taking orders from a woman . . .'

This was his idea of a joke; Valerie laughed dutifully, feigning outrage. But I didn't smile.

'I can't finish this, Val, it's too rich. Let's have coffee in the study.'

So we all went through to the inner chamber again. Valerie and I sat down in the same armchairs, my father settled himself behind the desk. He was pretending to be happy, but I could see that our conversation at the table had upset him. He was moving things around on the top of the desk, looking around the room, till finally his peevishness fixed on a point, and stayed there.

'Valerie. Those flowers. I've spoken to you already.'

'I keep telling the girl . . .'

'Well, tell her again, right now.'

'Just a moment, darling, till she brings the coffee.'

We sat in silence until one of the maids, an elderly woman, bare-foot and aproned, came in with a tray. While she poured, Valerie spoke sideways to her: 'Betty, the flowers . . .'

'Ma'am?'

'Don't you want to take them? They'd look so nice in your little room . . .'

'Ma'am.'

Betty carried the brown, limp leaves from the mantelpiece to the door.

'Betty!'

'Master?'

'You're dropping petals, Betty. All over the place. Please, please . . .'

And the old lady in the nice blue uniform set the dying flowers down and got on to her knees. She started crawling across the floor, picking up bits of flowers as she went.

'There, Betty,' my father murmured, pointing patiently, '. . . there . . . another one there . . .'

While I sipped the sour coffee, hearing the rim of the china cup clink against my teeth.

12

I came back in darkness, late at night. All the lights were out, except for at the front entrance and in the duty room. Framed by the window, I could see Laurence sitting at the desk inside, very upright and alert, his hands clasped in front of him. Wearing his white coat.

There was a lot of wind and he didn't hear the car. I sat for a long time watching him over the intervening gravel and grass. Neither of us moved. He seemed deep in thought, but I wasn't thinking anything particularly. I just wanted to see what he would do. But he didn't do anything.

I didn't go in to see him. I went straight to the room and got into bed, and my sleep was like a continuation of the numb momentum of the drive: a falling forward into a landscape that rushed perpetually past and into me.

I only woke when it was light and he was sitting on the other bed, looking at me. His face was tired, but his eyes were shining with a peculiar glow.

'What?' I said, sitting up. Something about his look alarmed me. 'What's the matter?'

'Nothing,' he said, smiling.

But he went on looking at me in that way.

'Oh, Frank,' he said at last. 'So much has happened since you left.'

'I've only been gone for two days.'

'Yes. But everything's different now.'

He was happy when he said this, despite the tiredness. And I will admit that his happiness perturbed me. But when I'd got myself out of bed and splashed some water on my face, the story that came out was not a happy one.

He'd thought a lot, he said, about what I had told him. About Tehogo and the stealing. It wasn't right that nothing should happen. And in the end he decided to do something.

'What did you do?'

He went to see Dr Ngema. He approached her in her room on the night that I left. And he told her the story of what had happened to me as if, in fact, it had happened to him. The knock on the open door, going into the room, seeing the bits of metal lying around.

He told me this blandly, with no expression, and I imagined this might have been the way he'd told it to Dr Ngema too. But when he'd finished talking he blushed suddenly, a hot red colour.

'What did she say?' I asked.

'She said, was I sure? How did I know where the metal came from? I said I was sure. She said, why did I go into Tehogo's room if he wasn't there?'

'She said that?'

'She said something about I had no right.'

'I didn't break in,' I said. 'It's not as if I picked the lock. Jesus.' A hot flush passed across my face too.

But his blush had gone and the happy smile was back. 'It was terrible, Frank,' he said. 'She called Tehogo in.'

'She called him in?'

'Well, it was like a farce. I was busy talking to her and there was a knock on the door and it was Tehogo, looking for something. So she said to him, you'd better come in. There's something serious we have to discuss.'

'And?'

'We sat there looking at each other, just like you're looking at me now. She made me tell the whole story again. He just kept shaking his head, like he knew I was lying. I was lying, Frank—that was the thing. It wasn't my story, it didn't happen to me. It felt like they both knew, they were listening to me and nodding and waiting, but they knew.'

'But they didn't know, Laurence. Oh, Jesus. What happened then?'

'Then he said, let's go and look. He got up, very calm, and we went with him to his room.'

'And?'

'And there was nothing there.'

I stared at him.

'Nothing,' he repeated sadly, still with that strange smile on his face. 'The room was a mess and everything, just like you said, but there was no metal or anything like that. I looked everywhere.'

'They moved it out,' I said. 'Tehogo and that friend of his. What-sisname, Raymond. They took it.'

'Maybe. But it was terrible, Frank. I just had to stand there and say, but it was here, I promise you, it was here. And they kept looking at me. I was lying, Frank, don't you see? I knew it myself, so they must've known too.'

'And?' I said. 'And?'

'Well, it was all over by then. Pointless, you know. There was a bit more talk—'

'What kind of talk?'

'We went back to Dr Ngema's office. There was a bit of discussion, this and that, and then Tehogo asked me why I'd gone to his room. What I wanted him for. And I just didn't know. I had nothing to say. What did you go there for, Frank?'

'Tapes.'

'Tapes?'

'It doesn't matter,' I said. 'Forget about it. Go on.'

'Well, there was no use pretending. We all just stared at each other. It was so horrible, that silence. I'd been caught out, you see.' He sat for a while, shaking his head, then went on in a different, lighter tone: 'So I told them. It was no good pretending any more. They could see.'

'You told them? Told them what?'

'That it hadn't been me who went into the room. That it was you. You saw the stuff, you told me about it . . . oh, all of it, I told them. I had to.' His smile was big now. 'I felt so much better afterwards, Frank. To get it all out in the open. It was the lying I couldn't take. It's not in my nature, What's the matter, Frank, what's wrong?'

The smile had gone. I was up and walking towards him. I think it was actually my intention to commit some action, but when I got close I veered away and stood staring out of the window. The same view, the overgrown yard with its ragged leaves, the peeling, blistered wall. I stared for a while, then I went back to my bed and sat down again, trembling.

'But it's sorted out, Frank,' he said. 'You don't need to worry. I explained everything to them.'

'Explained what exactly?'

'That it was me, the whole thing. Coming to Dr Ngema, telling the lie about what I'd seen—it was all my idea. I told them that. I told them that you weren't going to say anything, that you felt sorry for Tehogo. How I was the one who . . . But it's sorted out now, you don't need to worry. We even shook hands.'

'Who?'

'Me and Tehogo. I said I was sorry and we made it up. It's all sorted, Frank. No problem for you.'

Incredibly, his expression of dismay was gone and that smile was back again.

'What are you smiling about?' I said.

'Things are good, Frank. It's all worked out for the best. It always does, somehow.'

I didn't know what this meant. My mind was occupied else-where. And I was too distracted to focus on what else might have happened while I had been gone. This was big enough for now. But I was soon to find out more about Laurence's smile.

'You'd better go and see her,' he added quickly. 'She did want to talk to you.'

'Who?'

'Dr Ngema. It's just a formality, Frank, don't look so worried.'

I went to her office. She was working at her desk, but the moment she saw me she got up and closed the door conspiratorially. We sat in the low chairs, our knees almost touching.

'It's been a bit of a mess, Frank,' she said. 'But it's sorted out now, I think.'

Almost the same words he'd used. I didn't know what *sorted out* meant in all of this.

'I'm sorry, Ruth, for the part I played. But I had no idea—'

'No, of course not. It was his doing, he said so himself. But it almost caused a lot of trouble. It still might. He's a very impulsive young man.'

'What can I do to help?'

'You could keep an eye on him for me. I've come to an arrangement with him. But I want to be sure that he sticks to it.'

'What arrangement?'

'It's about his clinic. You know, the field-hospital thing that he did yesterday.'

My mind was scattered between so many points that this was the first time, since I'd left, that I'd thought of it.

'Yes?'

'It was very successful, apparently. The Santanders said . . . They seem very pleased.'

'And so?'

'I've told him he can have another one. To be honest, I've sort of indicated that we might continue with them on an ongoing basis. I don't think it'll come to that, of course. But I had to persuade him somehow.'

She was beaming—an unusual display of emotion for her—at her own cleverness.

'The next one will be in a month,' she went on. She named a village I'd never heard of. 'Listen to this, Frank. It all fits together.

The local government will be holding a function there that day. It's a big celebration, because they're delivering electricity for the first time. So I've arranged that we'll do the clinic the same day. There'll be lots of media, lots of speeches, lots of political attention . . . Good for all of us.'

'Brilliant,' I said. The word fell out of me dryly. 'And he accepts this as a . . . as a . . .'

'Trade-off? Yes. I think so. I didn't put it to him like that, of course. I said that he had to choose. If he wanted to push the case with Tehogo, then I would have to make a case against him. For lying. And that there'd be a whole inquiry, Tehogo might lose his job, Laurence might be suspended . . . Considering all that, I said I couldn't see a way for us to go on holding these clinics. On the other hand, I said, there was this opportunity . . .'

'And he accepted that,' I said again, incredulously.

'He had to. He can't make a case against Tehogo anyway. Only you can.'

After a short pause, in which I could hear the branches outside her window rubbing together, I said: 'And what if I do?'

She was astounded. The beaming expression was gone, her eyes and mouth widened into circles. 'Excuse me?'

'What if I pressed the case against him? Because I did see the stuff. It was there.'

The silence was long this time. Then she said, 'I don't understand. I thought you didn't want . . .'

'I'm not sure I do. But are you just going to leave it at that? He's stealing from you.'

'Well, I . . . yes. But he's been given a warning. He won't do it again. It's only bits of metal anyway. Nobody was using it. No harm done.'

'No harm done?' I shook my head. 'This is your hospital, Ruth. The bits of metal are part of your hospital.'

'I know that, Frank.' Something in her face was hardening now. 'Think of the alternative for a second. You've been waiting a long time to become head of the hospital. Things are moving now at last, it looks like it'll happen soon. Do you want to throw that away? If you start an inquiry at the Department of Health, it'll take months, it'll exhaust us all. The accusations that'll fly around, Frank, have you thought about that? The outcome is by no means clear. And at the end of the day it is, yes, it is bits of metal you're fighting about.'

'Surely not. Surely it's a principle that's at stake.'

'What principle is that?'

I was speechless. What principle was I fighting for? It seemed too obvious to have a name. But I was getting into something now that was too deep and difficult for me, and I decided to retreat.

'Anyway,' I said. 'This is all theoretical. Because I don't want to push the point.'

'I'm relieved to hear it, Frank. There's too much on the line. For everybody.'

'Yes. I do see that. So what is it you want me to do?'

I was speaking lightly and quickly now, as if none of the dangerous talk had happened, and she was answering me in the same way.

'Just make sure, if you can, that Laurence doesn't change his mind. You're a good influence on him, Frank. He listens to you.'

'Sure. I'll keep an eye on him.'

'Thanks. It's for your sake too.'

'I know that.'

But when I left her office I was full of confusion and contradiction and it was with an ache in my head that I went to sit in the recreation room. Laurence was sleeping, and this was normally a quiet refuge, but today it felt crowded. It was bright and loud in there. A music cassette was blaring and the Santanders were playing table tennis together. Themba and Julius were drinking coffee and talking.

'You want to play too, Frank?' Jorge called.

I shook my head. The game went on without me. In my stupor it felt to me that this movement and frivolity were the normal state of things and it was only my mood that excluded me. But at some point Claudia threw down the bat and came and sat next to me, laughing and sweating amiably.

'You come back today?' she said.

'Last night. Late.'

'You miss the clinic yesterday. Very good. Oh, very good time.'

'Yes,' Jorge said, coming up. 'We thought of you. We had a lot of fun.'

'Oh, very good,' Claudia repeated. 'So many people! So much talking! Oh, too much.'

'That's nice,' I said. No other words would come.

It was then it began to dawn on me that the light and happy mood in the room was new. The way that Claudia was sprawled there, talking easily to me—as if without rancour and resentment after our affair—was something she'd never have done just a few days before. And this fresh energy, so optimistic, so young, was connected to what had happened yesterday, while I was away.

I remembered the smile on Laurence's face, incongruous while he was telling his story. I was to see that same smile again a few days later, at the weekly staff meeting. The only item on the agenda was the clinic. And Dr Ngema set aside her caution for the announcement. It had been a resounding success, she said; if anyone doubted it, they had only to look at the new spirit amongst the staff. Although our material resources were thin, we had achieved something significant: we had reached out and touched the community, we had let them know we were here. And she had no doubt that people who'd never heard of the hospital before would be beating a path to our door.

While Laurence sat smiling at his shoes.

'Of course,' Dr Ngema said, 'that was just a try-out. The idea was to go on holding these clinics if the first one was a success. And I'm pleased to be able to tell you that there'll be a follow-up very soon.'

She looked around at us importantly. But I couldn't listen while she repeated the details of what she'd told me: the big government function where electricity was going to be delivered to poor people for the first time. The whole event was clear in my mind, as if it had already taken place—the mobs of people gathering, the shining face of Laurence at the centre of the audience. The talk, the long and pointless talk, most of it probably not understood; but that didn't matter. What mattered was that it happened—the symbolic value of it. What mattered was the spirit amongst the staff.

I stared at the dartboard behind the door, where a single dart, hanging by its tip, took on a luminous significance, and only came back to myself as Dr Ngema was saying, '. . . I don't need to tell you how important this is. Outreach work, community work . . . it's the kind of thing the previous regime didn't care about. We must all commit ourselves to the new way . . .'

Then applause, spontaneous, in which even Dr Ngema joined. The only people who sat watching were Tehogo and myself, silent and apart on opposite sides of the room.

Tehogo had always been silent, but his silence was different now. The anger, the accusation in it were palpable, and I thought they were directed at me.

I'd seen him once already since I got back from the city. But even before that I knew everything had changed. It was one chance encounter, one tiny gesture in the encounter, that showed me where I stood.

On the day that I got back, after I'd sat in the recreation room among the happy staff for a while, I went walking through the hospital grounds. Thoughts and impulses were boiling up in me, so that

I couldn't rest. I paced up and down, I stood with my fingers hooked into the bars of the gate, looking out. In the evening I decided to take a longer walk, through the town. And on my way out I passed Raymond, Tehogo's pretty friend, the young man I'd accused of being an accomplice. He was sitting on the low, crumbling wall at the edge of the parking lot, twitching one dangling foot, waiting. The last time I'd seen him he was at the party. He was well-dressed and neat; even in the dusk he was wearing dark glasses. I nodded to him to say hello, but when I was opposite him he raised one hand and drew a finger smilingly across his throat.

Just that, just the one gesture, but all the way into town I was shaking. Not from fear, or not entirely; something else. It was a gesture Tehogo was sending to me, it was what Dr Ngema hadn't quite spoken aloud in her office that morning: all the unsaid, un-done rage transplanted into the bored hand of this stranger.

When I came back he was gone. The little sagging wall was bare.

I went looking for Tehogo. It was supper-time and I found him in the dining-hall, sitting by himself at one end of the long table. Claudia Santander was also there with Laurence, and some of the electric buzz from that morning still went on between them on the far side of the room. But around Tehogo there was an angry halo. He'd finished eating and was sitting staring at the wall, his empty plate in front of him. When he saw me he seemed to need some activity to distract him and he picked up the salt cellar and started rolling it around in his hand.

I went to sit next to him. Laurence and Claudia glanced over at us, then went on with their intense conversation. I could hear something about Havana, something about a state medical programme.

Tehogo started to toss the salt from one hand to the other. Left, right, left.

'Tehogo.'

He said nothing. Went on throwing. I pulled my chair a bit closer to him.

'Can we speak?' I said. 'I want to explain what happened.'

Left, right, left.

'I know you're very angry. Hurt and angry. But it wasn't me who did this, Tehogo. If you'd just listen to me.'

He put the salt cellar down firmly and folded his arms, staring in front of him.

'You are not my enemy, Tehogo.'

Then he turned his head and looked at me. The stare lasted only a moment, before he pulled his chair back and got up. I think I actually clutched at him, to stop him, but he was already striding away. Out of the room, not looking back.

There was a brief pause, in which I could feel Laurence and Claudia watching me across the room. Then their conversation resumed, soft and urgent. I sat with my head in my hands, trying to think through all the words and images. *You are not my enemy, Tehogo.* Who was my enemy then?

So I had begun to understand what Laurence meant when he told me that everything was different now. In the two days that I'd been gone, my place in the hospital had changed. Nobody was speaking to me in quite the same way any more.

The change was tiny, but huge. It had no centre, no dimensions you could pin down, but it preoccupied and troubled me like a single, definable event.

It was a few days before I found out that something outside the hospital was different too. And this change would affect me more profoundly, maybe, than everything else.

Laurence didn't tell me at first. He let it all go by—the meeting with Dr Ngema, the talk with Tehogo, the Monday morning staff meeting. It was almost the middle of the week before he brought it up, casually, incidentally, as if it had only just occurred to him. And yet it was obvious, almost from the first syllable, that he'd been waiting to speak to me.

'Oh, yes . . . Frank . . . can I talk to you for a minute?'

We were in the room. It was one of those indeterminate times of day, with the light through the dusty window coming in grey and filtered, without heat.

He sat down on his bed and gazed at me. Then he got up and came over to my side.

'Is it okay if I sit here?'

'Go ahead.'

He sat next to me on the bed and I could hear his uneasy breathing for a while.

'How are you?' he said at last.

'I'm fine.'

'You don't look fine. Was it hard for you down in Pretoria?'

'Whatever you want to say,' I told him irritably, 'I wish you'd just say it.'

His breathing sounded painful, then he said, 'It's about the clinic. Well, no, it isn't. I mean, not the clinic as such. Connected with the clinic. In a way. But not the clinic itself, no.'

'I have no idea what you're talking about.'

He took a deep breath. 'All right. That woman.'

'What woman?'

'That one. You know. Your friend.'

And then I knew. 'You mean Maria.'

'Yes. Her. From the souvenir shop.' His eyes were on me, but when I looked at him they dropped, slid away.

'What about her?'

'After the clinic. When everybody was standing around. She came to talk to me. She said she had a big problem, could I help her.'

In the silence I understood, and the word hung between us in the air, waiting to be spoken.

'Pregnant.'

He nodded and swallowed; the sound was loud and distinct in the room.

'She wants you to get rid of it for her.'

He nodded again.

I felt calm. I felt unnaturally calm and still. I said to him, 'Why are you telling me this?'

He tried to speak, but no sound would come; and I saw in that moment he wasn't able to speak the truth. Instead he whispered, 'I want your ... your advice.'

'Abortion isn't a crime any more, Laurence. You're allowed to help her.'

'She ... she doesn't want it done here.'

'Where then?'

'Out there. In the shack.'

'But that's crazy.'

'I know. But she's terrified of something. Or somebody. She wants me to come there late at night. It has to be a secret.'

'Why?'

He shrugged, and all his desperation was there in the gesture. And none of his pride and confidence was left from the staff meeting a few days ago; he was just a confused young man, in need of help.

I said, 'What are you going to do?'

'I don't know.'

'By when must she ... ?'

'Soon. I'm not sure exactly when, but soon. Frank, isn't it possible ... ?'

'What?'

'Can't it ... can't you ... ?' He shrugged again.

'You're not asking me to do it, are you?'

He smiled painfully. 'I don't know. It crossed my mind. You ... you seem to know her.'

'But Laurence,' I said, 'she came to you.'

And it was true. If he hadn't held his little clinic, if he hadn't gone to that particular village, he would never have seen her again.

And part of me—a hard, cold place deep inside—felt satisfaction at his dilemma. He wanted to go out and make grand symbolic gestures for an audience, but the moment reality rose up he didn't know how to cope.

Of course I wasn't going to leave it at that. Of course I would find out what had happened, of course I would do something. But for the moment I was not without a certain grim pleasure at the hole Laurence had dug for himself.

I drove out that night to see her. I went without knowing what I was going to say. The last time I'd been here was before I left for the city, when I told her I'd be back the following night. But I hadn't gone back.

There was another roadblock set up on the way. When they asked me where I was going I said, 'Just for a drive,' but I could see that this answer perplexed the young soldier who'd pulled me over. He made me get out and open all the doors, so that he could search everywhere—under and between the seats, in the cubby-hole, in the boot, in the engine. The car was empty and he had to let me go, but it was with an obscure weight of guilt that I drove on, as if I was actually smuggling something secret and illegal.

And when I got to the shack the white car was parked outside. The white car, that might or might not have been outside the Brigadier's house. I couldn't stop. There was no point in waiting, but I decided to do what I'd said anyway and just go for a drive. I rode on for miles through the dark. Then at some point short of the escarpment I pulled over and got out. The night was warm, the sky crowded with stars. I sat on the hot bonnet of the car with the hissing wastes of grass around me, staring into the black.

It felt good to be there, away from everything, alone. For a little while my life felt like something separate to me, a hat or a shirt I'd dropped on the floor and could push at, meditatively, with my foot. And out of this sense of things, a strange dream came to me.

In this dream I went to Maria in her shack. She looked like she normally did, but she was wearing a shiny yellow dress, something I'd never seen. And I went to her and took her hands in a way I'd never done before. The feeling between us was warm and wordless, pushing action ahead of it like a wave.

I said to her, 'Maria, come with me.'

She was confused. She didn't know what I meant.

'Everything is possible,' I told her. 'Come with me.'

'But I must look after the shop.'

'No. I mean something different. I don't mean for a little while. I mean for ever. Come with me, away from here. We'll leave everything behind. Your job, my job. Your place, my place. We'll go to the city and get married and live together and everything will start again. From the beginning.'

She shook her head.

'Yes,' I said. 'It's true. Everything is possible.' And I saw that it was. I saw how simple such a huge change could be.

But then the dream shifted. She shook her head, and the colour of her dress was different, and the future slid by me in the warm dark and was gone. The wrong feeling, the wrong time: everything was too late. All the power went out of me and I climbed down from the bonnet and drove back.

The white car was still there.

When I got back to the hospital the world was fixed in its usual place, waiting. The dark buildings, full of disuse and emptiness. The room, with my tiny collection of possessions. Laurence Waters, asleep, his head flung sideways on the pillow.

I stood there for a long time, looking down at him. In the dim glow from an outside light his face seemed even younger than it was. Not young enough to be innocent, but soft and pale and vulnerable to violence. And the violence was in me: from nowhere it occurred to me how simple it would be to break a sleeping head like this. One hard, heavy blow with the right object and it would be done.

Because he was the enemy. I saw it now. The enemy was not outside, at large, in the world; he was within the gates. While I had slept.

Night thoughts; but nothing like this had come to me before. And it was terrible how casual, how very ordinary, the idea of murder could be. I turned away from it, and from myself, and went to bed.

13

But the night thoughts weren't confined just to the dark any more; they leaked into the normal daylight hours. I went about my usual routine, carrying out my duties and moving in the well-worn tracks of habit. But behind the visor of my face a stranger—not entirely unfamiliar, a dark brother who'd left home long ago—had moved in.

Of course he was only a temporary resident. I was tolerating his presence, not for long, a day or two, the duration of a rage; then I would evict him and become an honourable person again.

But in that day or two, which became three or four, then five or six, I watched Laurence wrestling with his dilemma. He brooded on it, he languished. And I became fascinated by the complexities of his agony, like the torments of a man who must solve some impossible equation.

Everything was hanging between two points, waiting. That was how it felt. And not just in our room: in the larger world too. Even the long streets of the town, when I drove or walked through them, felt charged with some imminent event. And in the little sites and places, too, that were the backdrop to my life, things weren't quite the same as before.

Mama Mthembu bought her pool table. I was in the supermarket in town one morning when I saw it go past on the back of a truck. By the time I went round for a drink that night it was installed in the bar. And a bunch of soldiers and strangers was hanging around, playing and watching, getting drunk.

The crowd that came to Mama's place was different lately. Maybe the soldiers had drawn them. A lot of the solitary figures hanging around were women, made up in tarty bright colours. I don't know where they came from—the villages near by, or over the border, maybe—but they were here to do business, and it wasn't long before truckers who plied the nearby main road were stopping too. That was new. So amongst the quiet, lost, familiar faces who used to head here for company, coarser faces were springing up. The atmosphere became looser and louder, jollier in a certain way, but also more violent. I was there on one occasion when a fight blew up out of nowhere—a hectic exchange of fists between a soldier and a trucker—then disappeared again, overtaken by the click of billiard balls and the jangle of loose change.

Then this strangeness, this violence, spilled over into the streets outside. One night there was a robbery in town. A gang of four armed men wearing balaclavas went into the supermarket. There were no customers inside at the time, but they beat up the manager and emptied the safe and drove down the main street, firing at the street-lamps. Nothing like this had ever happened before. The town had always been a place where boredom was a kind of violence, but for days afterwards the only talk was of the robbery, the gang.

The manager came to the hospital. He'd been pistol-whipped around the head, and I had to stitch up a deep cut above his eye. The man was in shock, and he kept telling the story over and over in broken phrases: how they'd just stepped in out of nowhere, faces blanked out.

'What kind of car were they driving?' I asked. 'Did you see?'

'I saw it clearly. A white Toyota.'

A white car. Was the one that stood outside Maria's shack a Toyota? I didn't know—the makes of cars were a foreign language to me—but the image became a kind of certainty in my head. Of course it meant nothing; there were thousands of white cars on the road. But for me it did mean something. And when I went out at night I was more watchful, more alert, than I had been before.

I didn't go back to Maria. I was waiting now to see what Laurence would do. When I went out at night it was down to Mama's place, and I didn't leave before I was drunk.

Colonel Moller was often there too. Like me, he sat on his own, in a shadowed corner somewhere. Like me, he was always watching. You could see the glitter of his eyes in the under-lit gloom, and one night he raised his glass to me in an ironical greeting.

It took me a while to realize that part of the reason I was going there was to see him. Night after night, usually alone. Not to speak to him, I didn't want that, but just to see his lean figure sitting still amongst the smoke and music and voices. Not a comforting sight—the memory he stirred up in me hurt like a broken bone—but one I somehow needed.

He wasn't always there, of course. On some nights all the soldiers were away. Then I knew that they were setting up their roadblock, searching cars, looking busy. But I wasn't the only one in town to wonder whether they ever did anything else. You saw them sometimes, driving up and down the main road in their jeep, very industrious, very fast. So much activity, so calibrated and intense: it had to mean something. But never once in all that time did I see them arrest anybody.

Not all the change was out there, far away; some of it was closer to home. Tehogo had always been unreliable, but now he started to miss work regularly. Two or three times over the next couple of weeks I found myself on duty with nobody around to assist me. And I heard the Santanders complaining about it at lunch one day too. But when Tehogo did come sauntering in, hours late, he didn't even try to excuse himself. There was just a shrug and, towards me, a surly silence full of words.

Nor did it help to go looking for him. On the third occasion I went to his room and knocked. But the door, this time, was locked, and the air on the other side felt unused and old. Hours later I saw him come in through the gate. By then I didn't feel like talking to him, but when he passed me a little later he smelled of sweat and his eyes were bloodshot and tired.

I tried to speak to Dr Ngema about it. But she wasn't too interested and the ghost of our earlier talk about Tehogo still hovered near by.

'He's working impossible hours, Frank,' she told me. 'He's doing the work of three people, remember.'

'I know that. But he hardly seems to be here any more.'

'He's having a hard time at the moment. Be patient, Frank. It'll all settle down.'

I didn't push it. Recent events were too close, and there were too many questions around me. I waited for somebody else to notice and complain, but it didn't happen. People were too distracted, maybe, caught up in the new buzz and thrill around the hospital.

Because it didn't go away. The excited feeling that Laurence had conjured up with his clinic seemed to linger long afterwards. I heard people talking at meal-times, or in the recreation room at night. There was a lot of discussion about the next clinic and what it might lead to.

One night, as we were getting ready for bed, Laurence said, 'She's decided to stay, you know. Claudia Santander. She doesn't want to go back to Cuba any more.'

'Oh, really. That's good.'

'There's a sort of programme with field clinics in Cuba that she's been telling me about. It sounds like we may be able to get something similar going here. She says she feels like she's discovered her purpose. In being here, I mean.'

'Good,' I said. 'It only took her ten years.'

That was the only way I could see it. All this energy and renewal: it had saved the Santanders' marriage. No matter that the world out there was still full of disease and calamity, as long as peaceful silence reigned on the other side of the wall.

One day when I was on duty an old man came in. He had a boy with him, a nephew or a grandson, who told me that the old man had been at Laurence's clinic. That was why, he explained, they'd come in today. Before that they didn't even know that the hospital existed.

He was all smiles, this old man, though he didn't speak a word of English himself. He seemed to have been touched by the same excitement that was running through the hospital corridors. But when it came down to an examination, it turned out that his complaint—a cataract developing in one eye—was something we weren't equipped to deal with here. He would have to go to the other hospital, the real and functioning one, over the escarpment. I wrote out a referral for him, addressing it to the young doctor, du Toit, I usually dealt with there.

The old man's face fell in confusion when I sent him away. But there it was: all the good feeling that: the clinic had generated running out into nothing.

I didn't tell Laurence about the old man. He might have taken it, in spite of everything, as a victory. But perhaps not. There was, in that waiting, hanging time, a heaviness to Laurence that hadn't been there before.

It was because of Maria, I knew that. He was trying to decide what to do. He didn't mention it to me again, but the question was between us all the time and he kept looking at me, at odd moments, to see what I thought. But I said nothing. I still had every intention of doing something, taking some action, but I wanted to push things to the point where Laurence's easy rules would break.

Then one day he collected a few basic instruments and utensils together. He didn't make a show of it, but he wanted me to see him. He got a big bowl and a cake of soap from the kitchen. A clean sheet from the linen cupboard. He laid out a pair of gloves, a speculum, a catheter, a cervical dilator, on his bed, as if he was carrying out an inventory. Then he sat down on the windowsill, his chin on his knees, and looked out.

I understood that he'd made his choice, and now he was offering one to me. There was still time. I could stop him. Up to the final moment, when he walked out of the door, I could still hold up a hand and say, *Wait, Laurence. Let me go instead.* Or: *Don't do it, Laurence. Let me speak to her first.*

But many days had gone by and I hadn't spoken to her, and this day was going by and I didn't stop him; and I knew now that I would let it be. What I'd said was the truth: she'd spoken to him, not to me. And the child, after all, was probably not mine; and if it was, this was probably the only answer in any case. There was nothing I could do to change the course of events. So I watched him and said nothing.

Later that night he collected everything together, moving slowly, like a person in pain. He put on his white coat. Then he walked to the door and stopped.

'Frank.'

'Yes?' I said, speaking too fast and too loud.

'What are you doing tonight?'

'I'm not sure. I think I'll just hang out. I'm tired.'

'If you feel like it, we could go out later. For a drink or something.'

'Where? To Mama's? I was there last night, I don't know if I can face it again.'

'Oh. Okay.'

'And I'm tired. Let's see how we feel.'

'Okay.'

I didn't look up, but I could sense when the doorway was clear. He'd gone. I sat for a little while and then I went to the window to watch his lonely figure cross the car park to his car and drive out slowly into the dark.

He was gone a long time. Three or four hours at least. I felt nothing, but I could observe from my own behaviour that feeling was loose in me somewhere. I walked up and down the tiny square of floor like some kind of big, predatory animal in a cage. Later I got into bed and turned off the light, but there was no possibility that I would fall asleep.

I heard his car come back, turn in at the gate and stop. I heard the car door and his footsteps coming, slow and heavy, along the path.

When he opened the door I lay still, but he showed no interest in me. His bag seemed to be loaded down with stones. And he was like a man who'd carried stones a long way. He bumped into his bed, said something to himself in the dark, went into the bathroom. I could hear the water running and running, the sound of him washing himself over and over.

I got up and put the light on again. It was a still and airless night, warm with returning summer, and I felt suddenly how hard it was to breathe. I went and opened the window, knelt on his bed for a while to feel air on my skin.

When he came back in he was naked and still dripping with water. He looked at me and went over and sat on my bed, facing me. Neither of us said anything for a long time. I was in my underwear, and with both of us so stripped down in the disarray of the room, it was as if we were lost in some labyrinthine intimacy. But his face, which was dark and different, was like the face of a stranger to me.

It was only afterwards that I realized: the quality, whatever the quality was, that had given his face its distinction, was gone.

He said, 'Why have you done this?'

It was an odd question.

I said, 'But I've done nothing. I've been here the whole time.'

'Yes.' He nodded, and it felt that something else would follow, but nothing did.

Then it came. Not from him; from me.

'If you want to blame somebody,' I said, 'blame yourself. We were all okay here. It was all going along fine. Then you came. And you couldn't leave everything as it was. No, you had to make it better.

You had to sort it out, improve life for everybody. Now see where we are.'

'Where are we?'

'Exactly where we were. Except that none of us feels okay any more.'

'I don't think we're where we were. It is better than before. I'm not sorry about that.'

'Because of one little clinic in the bush.'

'Is that what you think?'

'I wasn't there. But I know. What did you achieve? Nothing. Talk, talk, talk. A lecture about Aids. A lecture on hygiene and health. For God's sake, Laurence. Those people need drugs and treatment, but of course they're not available. All you can give them is talk.'

'It's just a beginning. Other things will follow.'

'What will follow? Another clinic in a few weeks. Along with electricity.'

'Do you think electricity means nothing? That's because you've never lived a day without it in your life.'

'I don't think it means nothing. But the fact that one tiny village is getting it means nothing. It's a sop, it's a symbol. It's like your medicine, Laurence. There are still millions of other people out there who aren't being helped. Do you really think talk and a few bright lights will save the world?'

'How will you change anything by doing nothing?'

'You can't change the way things are.'

'Of course you can!'

We looked at each other with astonishment and loathing.

'They're right about you,' he said slowly. It was a bitter realization. 'I couldn't see it before. But now I see.'

'What do they say about me?'

'That you're not part of . . . of the new country.'

'The new country,' I said. 'Where is it, this new country?'

'All around you, Frank. Everything you see. We're starting again, building it all up from the ground.'

'Words,' I said. 'Words and symbols.'

'It isn't. It's real. It's happening.'

'I don't think so.'

'Why? Why are you like you are?' It was an angry question, but he didn't sound angry. He sounded curious and sad. 'You're not a bad man.'

'Maybe I am.'

'You're not a bad man. But you say no to everything. It's written on you. I don't know what's happened to you. You just don't believe in anything. I don't think you even believe what you're saying now.'

'I do believe it.'

'That's why you can't change anything. Because you can't change the way you are.'

'Do you think it's so simple? At the middle of your life there's just one word, yes or no, and everything follows from that?'

'Maybe it is like that.'

I looked at him, but I didn't see him. I was seeing something else. A picture had come to me, and it was of Laurence and me as two strands in a rope. We were twined together in a tension that united us; we were different to each other, though it was in our nature to be joined and woven in this way. As for the points that we were spanned between—a rope doesn't know what its own purpose is.

The image stayed for a moment, then it went again, but we had both fallen quiet by then. All the high emotion was receding; he looked tired and grey. After a minute he rolled over and pulled the sheet over him. I waited a while, then put off the light and also lay down. We were in the wrong beds, but somehow that didn't feel so strange.

I was also weary now, my bones full of sand, but sleep took a long time to come. Everything that had just been said was wrong; it was the wrong conversation; it had nothing to do with the real business of the evening. And yet it was also the only real, the only possible talk.

In the morning it was past. When he got up the weight he'd carried in with him last night was gone. He moved quickly around the room, whistling through his teeth. When I sat up he grinned at me.

'Morning, Frank. Sleep okay?'

It was as if last night hadn't happened for him. I was the heavy one now. The weight had moved from him to me; some subtle exchange had taken place in the night. I was older and bigger and slower than before.

And I was thinking now, really thinking, about what had happened last night. In my mind I saw him again, crossing the car park in the dark. But my mind went further now: to the long road unrolling in the headlamps, taking him to the little wooden hovel under the trees . . . and inside.

It was only now, too late, that I thought about Maria. Somehow the whole thing had been about Laurence until now; she was on the side somewhere, an abstract problem I couldn't solve. But she wasn't abstract today; she was solid and warm and real, a human body I had lain with. And I had done nothing to help her.

I was on duty; I had to get dressed. But Laurence was also dressing, briskly and seriously, as if he had somewhere to go.

'What are you doing?'

He stopped, his shirt half-buttoned. 'I'm going out there.'

'Where?'

'You know where.' He wasn't looking at me now as he finished doing up his shirt. 'I said I'd check on her today.'

'You can't go now. There'll be people . . . It's the daytime.'

'But I'm on duty tonight.'

'I'll do it.'

'I told her I'd be—'

'I'll do it, Laurence.'

The note in my voice froze us both. He stared at me, then shrugged and looked away.

The hours of duty stretched idly away, and I thought only about her. When I came back to the room in the evening it was too early to go to Maria. Instead I did something odd. I cleaned the room. I went into town and bought detergents and soaps and cloths; then I came back and scrubbed and scoured the floors and walls and windows. Every corner. Afterwards I felt better for a while, as if an offensive mark somewhere had been erased.

But I couldn't sit quietly and when I went out in the car it was still early, too early to go to Maria, and so for an hour or two I drove around the town. Empty streets, the dark sockets of the lamps, the blank blind eyes of windows watching me. Then it was time and I headed out along the road.

When I got to the bluegum trees I turned off and stopped almost exactly where the white car had been parked a few nights ago, my headlamps angled away from the road. But they shone on dust and bush and empty air; the shack was gone.

14

For a few moments it seemed possible that I was in the wrong place. But when I got out of the car the outline of the shack was visible: a square paler than the surrounding soil, like the mark of a plaster on sunburned skin. A few loose planks and bits of plastic lay around.

Everything had happened here. On this little patch of sand. It had felt like a whole world, and now I saw it was just any piece of bush. In two weeks it would be covered again by weeds and thorns and grass.

The dust I'd kicked up drifted like smoke in the headlamps. I walked away from the light, along the little footpath to the village. It was a distance of twenty or thirty steps, but I'd never walked it before. As I got closer a dog barked at me; another took up the sound, and it was accompanied by this angry chorus that I made my entrance into the naked circle of earth at the heart of the village. The little mud houses ringed me around. It was all dust and dung and the ash of old fires; it was what I knew it would be.

Nobody was around. No lights were burning and the only movement was the dogs, skulking closer. I stood there as if somebody was coming to meet me. But I had never been so alone.

I knew then that she could be anywhere. She could be five steps away from me, in one of those houses, or in any one of the countless little villages scattered in the bush. Or she could be under the ground, in a shallow grave. For me, she had fallen off the edge of the world.

The anguish that rolled down then was like the first feeling ever to touch me: its rawness, its power, was almost like love.

The dogs were coming closer. I was an intruder. I didn't come, like Laurence Waters, in the daytime, with medicine and good advice; I came in out of the dark with the snarling of skeletal dogs for company. And there was nothing to be done except hurry back along the path to my car and drive back to town.

I drove at a wild speed. It was as if I was rushing to keep some assignation, but there was nowhere to get to, no destination at the end of the road.

Unless it was the hospital room, with Laurence sitting up in bed, writing something on a piece of paper.

He glanced up at me. 'Hello,' he said, sounding preoccupied. 'I'm planning.'

'Planning?'

'My clinic. Never mind. Oh, wow, I almost forgot!' He looked sharply up at me. 'How is she doing?'

'She's doing all right,' I said, turning my face away from him. He must've seen how I felt and thought he understood the reason, but he didn't understand.

In the morning I went back to the village. I parked next to where the shack had been; I walked the little footpath again. And now there were people: children playing, a woman shelling beans in a doorway, two old men deep in conversation. In the mud a fat pig lolled and the same dogs from last night started up out of the shade, barking.

I hoped to see a familiar face, the woman who brought food or water to Maria, somebody I knew. But no. And the man I did speak to, who was the only person I could find who spoke English, didn't know much about Maria. Yes, the shack had stood there. But now it was taken down. He thought the people had gone there somewhere, over there. He gestured at the blue hills in the distance.

Yes, yes, some of the older women sighed in agreement. They had gone over there.

Did they know Maria, I asked. Was any of them her friend?

But I could see in their puzzled faces that they hadn't heard the name. It was as I'd thought: her real name was something different, something she hadn't told me.

I didn't have much hope, but I made a little speech. If any of them could find Maria, I said, if any of them sent her to me, I would pay a reward. I took my wallet out to show them.

'Who are you?' the young man, my translator, asked me.

'My name is Frank Eloff. I'm a doctor. I work at the hospital in town.'

At this their baffled faces broke into smiles. There was a buzz of talk around me. The hospital! The clinic! And the memory of that recent event set loose a happy spirit amongst them, similar to the new mood amongst the staff at the hospital.

I'd almost forgotten. But of course it had happened here. And I heard one of the old women, who couldn't otherwise speak a word of English, say 'doctor Laurence, doctor Laurence' with a toothless grin of pleasure.

When I got away from them, back to the hospital, the weight in me had altered shape a little. Yes, it was Maria I was looking for, but her absence had spilled over into other, adjoining areas. For the first time the things I had done and said over the last few days began to look like a kind of madness. And the dark stranger in my head, who was so easy to blame for everything, seemed less separate from me than before.

It went on through the long, hot afternoon. Laurence was out somewhere and I lay, sweating on my bed, thinking. I felt my guilt towards Maria as a massive neglect and blindness. I was wretched. And what I'd done, or failed to do, to her, was no different in the end from what I'd done here, closer to home. In the hospital. In this room.

When Laurence came in, it was fully dark. This was hours later, but I hadn't moved from the bed. He put the light on and stared at me in amazement. 'What are you doing?'

'Nothing.'

'Why was the light off? Were you asleep?'

'No, I was thinking about things.'

'About what things?'

It was a huge effort for me to swing my legs over and sit up. Then nothing further would come.

Laurence stared at me. 'What?'

All of it rose against my teeth, a pressure that couldn't be released, and so I said nothing. In the silence I shook my head.

He smiled at me, his broad face gleaming like a badge. 'You shouldn't sit by yourself so much, Frank, it makes you depressed.'

'Laurence . . .'

'I haven't got time now. I've got to shower quickly, then I'm going out with Jorge and Claudia for a drink. Want to come?'

'No.' He was closed to me. I wanted to talk quickly, to say as many words as possible in the hope that one of them would be the right one, the word to absolve me, but he was already moving away, through the bathroom door. 'Laurence.'

'*Ja*?' He stopped, looking back, then he shook his head. 'Hey, relax, Frank, it doesn't matter.' He went through the door.

I sat on the bed, hearing the water splash and run. But it didn't wash anything away.

15

I went to look for her. Or so I told myself, though any noble motives fell quickly away. This particular memory is grainy and formless as a dream. I'm not even sure whether it was that night, or on one of the nights that followed. But I see myself sitting on the bed, with Laurence still washing himself next door in the bathroom, while my misery plucked me in different directions, until a sudden clearness came to me.

I see myself driving out of town. But that is a false image, made from all the other nights I drove that road. In fact, I walked. The reason is logical and obvious: a car parked any-where along that stretch of road would have drawn undue attention to itself. So I hurried along the gravel verge in the still, warm air, with the forest on both sides and the lights of the town disappearing quickly behind me.

Real memory only begins when I came to the turn-off on the left. I had passed it a few hundred times: the overgrown dirt track that led through the bush to the old army camp. Though I slowed, almost as a ritual, every time I came to the place in the road from where that camp was visible, I had never once gone there. I don't know why. I told myself it was a pointless spot to visit—abandoned and ugly, why bother? But the real reason was deep in me, and I felt it now, as I started down the track, as a line of fear that I was crossing for the first time.

I wasn't thinking about Maria any more. I wasn't thinking about very much at all. My attention, heightened and whetted by alarm, was on the darkness pressing in from all sides. The trees felt obser-vant and old. Grass was growing through the compacted ground underfoot. The night was like a lens in which my every movement was magnified for the attention of some enormous eye.

The track dipped down to a shallow stream burbling over stones, then climbed towards a ridge. The top of the ridge was a jumble of trees, till at a certain angle the leaves gave way to the outer fence of the camp. I could see a delicate tracery of wire, repeated and exact, against the sky. Near by was a tall pole that used to support a floodlight. But now the pole leaned companionably against a tree, its top weighted down with creepers.

I could see the main gate. If there was a sentry anywhere he would be here. I moved to the right, up a steep slope, towards the top of the ridge. This way I would avoid the obvious dangers, but as I slid and stumbled on stones, with branches grazing my face and hands, I felt how ill-equipped I was for this role of macho hero in the dark. I saw my true self, soft and overweight, in the light and warmth of Mama's place, drinking whisky and talking to Laurence, and the distance between that vision and me was the rupture that had torn through the middle of my life. Who was I, what was I doing here? A strangled sob of exertion came out of me as I clawed over the top of the ridge at last, and found myself just outside the wire, on the edge.

All that was left of the camp was three or four tents, sagging and shapeless, made of shadow more than form. Between them was open ground, with what looked like pieces of disused machinery. But no movement, no human figures anywhere. I don't know what I expected—soldiers around a big fire, the white car parked near by. Maria tied to a tree with a gag on her mouth. Though the inky stillness was perhaps more menacing. For a long time I couldn't move, pinioned in the cross-hairs of the silence, while my sweat dried to a cold second skin.

I had to go in. The big circle of dead ground was pulling at me. But it was like moving through deep water to force my legs to work. Numbness muffled me, and it was in a slow-motion parody of stealth that I crept down the fence to a place where it had collapsed. And stepped through. Then I stood still again, listening. But the only sound was the cacophony of my own heart and breath.

I relaxed a little then. If something was going to happen, it would probably have happened by now. The truth of this place was just absence and desertion. And I moved on, feeling lighter and easier, past one tent, and another, into the empty arena of gravel.

A little breeze had started. The few strands of grass quivered. The nearest tent gave off a sighing sound. But I wasn't frightened now; these were the normal vibrations of the forest at night.

And then something moved. Right in front of me, when I'd stopped looking for it. I didn't see it, I sensed it: a sudden little burst, a flexing of the dark. It had a will and life of its own. And in a second all my terror was back. Everything I most feared and dreaded, all the phantoms of the mind, had drawn together into a knot—a presence that had risen out of the dark.

I fell backwards on to the ground, but I was already up and outrunning thought before I could think it.

The mirror showed an ashen, frightened man to me. My clothes were filthy, covered in burrs and thorns. My skin was silty with dust and on my forehead a cut gleamed brightly.

I stood under the shower for a long time. The hot water calmed me and afterwards, as I dried myself and dressed in clean clothes, it was like taking on the normal world again. And as my mind evened out, it began to question what it had seen. Nothing, really—a sudden flurry in the dark. It could have been a buck or some other night animal, startled by my unexpected approach. Or maybe just a burst of wind.

These rational possibilities calmed me more. But underneath them, down at the core, the irrational terror remained. If I put my memory to it, I could relive that primitive instant.

I left the light on until I fell asleep. But Laurence was there when I woke up and for the first time his clothes, strewn around untidily on the floor, were a comforting sight to me. And the daylight, so steady and warm, made the whole expedition feel insane. None of it was substantial any more and the only tangible evidence was that sore place on my forehead.

'Where did you get that cut?' Laurence said when he woke up a bit later in the day.

'I bumped it on the medicine cabinet.'

'Bad one,' he said, and that was all.

If it was true, I had just changed the truth. A few words, and the whole thing went away.

But I was troubled the whole day. I was on duty and the vacant corridors were like a screen on which my mind replayed its images. No patients came in that day. Not one. And Tehogo didn't turn up for duty either. I was alone, encircled by hours and hours of time. When evening came I was weary, tired out by boredom, and for once it was easy to fall asleep.

In the morning the cut on my forehead had formed a scab. It was starting to heal. And when I went back on duty, I could work up some anger that Tehogo still wasn't there. I went looking for him this time, but his room was locked again and my knocking had a hollow sound to it.

He wasn't there the next day either. Or the next. And soon everybody knew it as an established fact: Tehogo had gone.

At the next staff meeting I tried to bring it up. What was the plan, I wanted to know, with Tehogo? Was he going to be replaced? Would we have to struggle on without assistance?

Dr Ngema still wasn't too interested. 'Um, well, for the time being, yes,' she said. 'He may still come back.'

'Come back?'

'He's been unreliable lately. We all know that. He might've just gone off by himself for a while.'

'And you'd take him back after that?'

'Well, yes. I would. Otherwise . . . what? You want me to adver-tise his post? We'd never get a trained nurse.'

'Tehogo never qualified anyway.'

'Yes, but he knew his job. A new person would have to learn everything from scratch. And it's not as if there's a lot to be done. We're managing.'

There was a note of irritation in her voice. Dr Ngema and I had never spoken like this to each other before, certainly not in public. I looked around at the other doctors, but they dropped their eyes. This wasn't a fight that anyone else felt strongly for.

'Just on principle,' I said, trying one last time. 'Why would you take him back after he's behaved like this? I mean, he's let us all down.'

'He has,' she agreed, then looked directly at me. 'But he's been having a hard time lately, Frank. You know that.'

You know that. The accusation silenced me, and I let the whole thing drop. It felt to me that everybody knew why I was trying to push the point: because now, at long last, in the most offhand of ways, Tehogo's room had become available.

It wasn't mentioned again. And in truth, I didn't think much about Tehogo's room any more. It had become almost irrelevant, a side issue. There were only a few months more before Laurence's year of community service was done, and then he would be gone again, and I would be left. Alone.

Then there was another robbery in town. This time it was the ser-vice station at the top of the main street. It was the same scenario as before: the gang of masked men in a white car, driving off into the dark.

The story was everywhere before the next day had started. But now theories and conjectures had attached themselves. The most compelling one was that the robbers were, in fact, some of the soldiers who were stationed in town. Somebody had talked to somebody who knew one of them who had told him . . . By midday this particular version had acquired the solidity of fact.

There had been a change of attitude lately towards the soldiers. When they first arrived their presence seemed like a sign of renewed life for the town. But as time went by, they looked less like saviours and more like a bunch of loud and arrogant and idle young men. People resented them. There had been a few altercations and incidents with local shopkeepers, and there was the general roughness in Mama's place at night. So it was perhaps inevitable that fear would turn inside-out and direct blame on them.

But I knew that it wasn't the soldiers. And now my own fear was compelling me to action. I went down to Mama's place on the night following the second robbery. That wasn't unusual, I was frequently there, but I confess that I went with an intention that was already half-formed.

I don't know what would have happened if there hadn't been an opportunity, a moment. Maybe I wanted the usual chaos and confusion, so that I could continue to dither on the edge of doing something. But the opportunity did come. When I first arrived there was no sign of Colonel Moller. A few of the soldiers were around, but that was all. Then, after a few hours and drinks had passed, and the place was a lot fuller than earlier, a break in the crowd showed his long figure to me.

He was sitting in a chair close to the pool table, watching a game. His back was to me. I could see his neck and the straight line of his haircut. He wasn't in uniform tonight. He was wearing jeans and a blue T-shirt, with some kind of smiling cartoon face on the back. I watched the blond hairs on his arm change colour in the light as he lifted his drink and set it down, lifted it and set it down. Otherwise he didn't move.

It was a while before I talked to him. I was trying to work up the courage. There was a perverse comfort in being so close to him, close enough to study the sunburn on his ears, while he seemed unaware of me. But then the crowd started to thin out again and I thought he might move away and the moment would be lost.

I went up close and spoke into his ear. 'I know something,' I said.

He turned quickly to look at me. 'What was that?'

'If you want to find what you're looking for,' I told him, 'go to the old army camp outside town.'

Then I left, walking fast. It was easy, in that crowd, to disappear from view in a moment. And that was what I wanted: a rapid exit, after a mysterious pronouncement.

I thought he wouldn't know me. Why would he, in a bar full of colourful characters and transients? I thought of myself as invisible, nondescript. But as I turned in through the hospital gates a pair of headlamps swung in behind me and his jeep slewed to a stop near by.

Now I was embarrassed and afraid. This was the conversation I didn't want, in the last place I would have chosen. I got out of my car and strode up to him, trying to recover some lost power through confrontation.

But he only seemed amused. He didn't climb down from his seat, but sat swaggeringly above me, a faint smile on his lips.

'What did you say to me, Doctor? I didn't quite catch it.'

'How do you know who I am?'

'I've seen you around. Not a lot of whiteys in this place. I asked about you.'

I looked up at him, but I couldn't hold his stare and dropped my eyes. It was like being transported backwards, to that lost little camp on the border. I was instantly afraid of him, as if all the intervening years hadn't happened. He was older and baggier than before; some of the clean, hard lines were blurred. But it was something else in him, something deeper than his face, that scared me. He was drawn in on a hard, tiny centre of himself, in the way of people who live in devotion to a single idea. In a monk this can be beautiful, but in him it was not.

I said, 'You are looking for the Brigadier.'

'The Brigadier?'

'Come on. You know who I'm talking about.'

He shook his head, looking puzzled. 'If you mean the darkie who used to run the show here . . .'

'Yes, I do.'

'But he's long gone, Doctor. Why would I be looking for him?'

'I thought you were here to plug up the border. I thought you were trying to stop people crossing over.'

'Maybe.'

'Well, he's your man. The Brigadier is your man. He runs the operation. Illegal traffic from the other side. Ivory, drugs, people. Everybody knows that. And I'll tell you something else. It's his guys that have pulled the two numbers here in town. The supermarket and the garage. And I know where they are.'

I'd been drinking for a while and the words, now that they'd started, were flowing loosely out of me. But there was no change of expression in his face. He was watching me with the same wary alertness, his blue eyes unblinking.

'Who told you this, Doctor?'

'Everybody knows.'

He gave a little smirk. 'And you think I'll find him in the old army camp.'

'Yes.'

'Did you see him there, Doctor?'

'No, I didn't see him. But I know he's there.'

'How do you know?'

'I can't explain, Commandant. But I know.'

He corrected me softly. 'Colonel.'

This little slip made me blush. But I could see that he wasn't interested. He'd followed me here out of curiosity, but he'd decided that I was a crank, somebody he could dismiss with a sigh and a shrug.

I said, 'Will you go and check it out?'

'Maybe.'

'There is something else . . .'

'*Ja?*'

'There might be a woman there. With them. She mustn't be hurt, Colonel. She isn't part of it all.'

'A woman?'

'With a man in a white car.'

He stared at me and nodded, but even through the icy colouring of his eyes I could feel his disdain. He had left the warm inside of the bar for a mad conversation in a car park. He turned the keys in the ignition.

I clutched his arm. 'It's true,' I said. 'Go and see.'

'The Brigadier is dead. There is no brigadier. Except me—in a few years, Doctor, I will be a brigadier.'

'He isn't dead,' I cried, and I leaned towards him, pushed by the force of everything I knew. It all threatened to spill out of me. But his arm was wrenched suddenly out of my grip as he put the jeep in gear and pulled away. I watched his headlamps float and fade, with the stirred dust dry in my mouth.

And maybe he was right. In this moment of vacancy I didn't feel sure of anything any more—even whether I'd actually been to the camp last night. Maybe I wanted it to be full of ghosts. Maybe I needed to believe in the Brigadier, with the past pinned to his chest, clinking faintly when he moved. Tending his mid-night flowers. Using my bones for fertilizer.

16

Tehogo came in the next day. I wasn't there; in the late after-noon I went back to the village behind Maria's shack to find out if there was any word of her. There wasn't, and in a melancholic frame of mind I took a drive all the way to the escarpment. I got back to the hospital in the evening, when it was already dark. All the lights were burning in the main wing, so that the building was very bright, and I could see figures moving in the windows.

I hurried in. The office was empty. I could hear activity next door, in the surgery, but when I started down the passage they were already coming out—Dr Ngema, the Santanders, and Laurence.

Nobody spoke to me. There was an air of distraction and wild-ness, everything out of control. But in a little while the frenzy seemed to settle. The Santanders were babbling together in Spanish, Dr Ngema was writing out clerking notes in the office. For a few minutes Laurence was floating, like me, in the lurid void of the corridor.

He said to me, 'What's going on?'

'I was hoping you could tell me.'

'I don't know, I don't understand it.'

'But what's happening?'

'He's down there. He's been shot in the chest. I don't think he's going to make it. Dr Ngema tried to operate, but it's too close to his lungs. I think—'

'Who? Who are you talking about?'

He stared incredulously at me, as if I was the inexplicable ele-ment in the scene. 'Tehogo,' he said at last. 'Where have you been?'

Even then I didn't understand. And then I did.

I went down the corridor. In the middle of the surgery, under the blue sepulchral glow of the night-lights, Tehogo lay on his back, a sheet up to his waist. He was on the ventilator, with an intravenous drip in his arm. His torso was bare, except for bandages and padding. And his face, when I bent over him, was collapsed inwards on its bones, as if he was already dead.

I went back up the passage. I said to Laurence, 'Who brought him in?'

'That other guy. That friend of his. I think.'

'You think?'

'I wasn't looking. It happened so quickly.' He put a hand to his head and I could see that he was on the edge of tears. I'd never seen Laurence cry before. 'I was on duty in the office and I heard a car come in outside. Very fast. Then the hooter went—over and over. I ran out. And the guy, whoever he was, the driver, was pulling Tehogo out the back.'

'What kind of car?'

'Sorry?'

'What kind of car was it?'

'I don't know, Frank, I wasn't looking, I'm sorry.' Now a tear did break free and run down, but his voice stayed steady. 'I took hold of Tehogo and started pulling him too, just to help, you know. But next thing the guy had got back into the car and was driving off hell for leather. I don't know, Frank, I think it was his friend, but I can't be sure. Why has this happened? What's going on?'

'I don't know,' I said. But I did know, as certainly as if I'd seen it.

I drove to Mama's place. It was still early and the bar was almost deserted. Mama was at the bar, counting stacks of small change into plastic bags. She smiled when she saw me.

'I'm looking for Colonel Moller.'

The smile faded; she'd seen something in my face. 'He's upstairs. In his room.'

'What number?'

She told me, and I climbed the stairs. It was the last door in the passage, on the corner of the building. He answered almost immediately when I knocked, as if he'd been waiting. But his wooden face betrayed a tiny tremor when he saw me; just for a second, then it was gone.

He was in uniform today. Camouflage pants, brown boots. But he'd taken off his shirt and the upper half of his body, smooth and almost hairless, seemed unrelated to the uniform below. Behind him I caught a glimpse of the room, like the one Zanele had stayed in down the passage. But the nude austerity of it had been hardened, if that was possible, by his presence. In the cupboard I saw his clothes piled up in rigorous vertical stacks. There was a disassembled rifle lying on the table, all its component parts laid out in neat, gleaming rows.

'Could I come in for a second, Colonel?'

He shook his head. 'If you don't mind, Doctor, I'm busy now. You'll have to talk to me at the door.'

Very polite, very distant. And I have no doubt that he used the same level tones with the people he'd tortured and killed. There was nothing personal in it for him.

'Colonel,' I said. 'We have a wounded man at the hospital. I think you know who he is.'

He gazed calmly at me, waiting.

'I want to know what happened to him.'

'I'm sorry.' He shook his head again. 'I wish I could help you, Doctor.'

He was still polite and opaque, but his attitude to me today was different. Last night I was just a loon, someone who could be brushed off with contempt. But now he was wary. His detachment had an element of power, a guarded watchfulness that was part of a game. He took me seriously now, though he was giving nothing away.

I said, 'Let me talk plainly. You don't have to tell me anything. But I know. I know you shot that man—you or your men. You went to the army camp, because I told you to go. You didn't think you'd

find anything, but you did. And something happened, somebody
ran, or fired a shot—and this is where it's ended up.'

He kept on staring at me, looking politely interested.

'Colonel,' I said, and the note of anguish was audible to us both.
'Can you not understand that I feel responsible? I am not here to
blame you, or make trouble. I only want to understand. I told you
where to go. I didn't think anything would happen, but now it has
happened. I am the reason for this. I know that. Not you, me. It
will help me to know what happened. That's all I'm asking. Please
help me, Colonel. Please.'

'I'm sorry, Doctor.'

'All right. Tell me this, then—just this one thing. Was anybody
else hurt? What happened to the others? Did they get away? Did
you arrest them?'

'I can't answer your question.'

'All right then. Forget about them—forget all of them. Just one
person: the woman. The woman I told you about last night. Was
she there? Is she safe?'

'I don't know.'

'Just one word, Colonel. Yes or no. Not even a word—just nod
or shake your head. Is she alive or is she dead? That's all I ask.'

He stepped back and closed the door. All the dialogue came
down to the finality of this single gesture. I rested my forehead
against the wall for a while, then went back down the passage.

The hospital had gone still and quiet again, but somehow the air
of commotion hung over it like a fog. Laurence and the Santanders
were still sitting around in the office. The talk was all about Tehogo.
The general opinion was that he would die.

I went to see him again. He was still in the surgery, still hooked
up to the machinery that was keeping him going. He seemed to be
half-made from synthetic materials and the human half was inert
and passive.

I said his name. But there was not the slightest response. So I stood and looked at him, at his face. I noticed a birthmark, a slightly darkened patch, on one cheek. A tiny crescent scar on his forehead. These were details I had never seen before, until this moment. And though I had lived and worked for years of my life close to him, I think I can say that this was the first time that my life felt connected to his.

17

Through the next day, although I wasn't on duty, I found myself going over several times to the main block to check on him. I wasn't doing this as a doctor, but out of some more personal need that couldn't be expressed in words. Each time it was the same: I stood at the bottom of the bed, staring and staring at him. Even now I don't know what I was looking for.

On a couple of occasions Dr Ngema was also there. As agitated and disturbed as I was, she was fussing around the bed, checking his pulse, his pupils, his blood pressure. No other patient had ever got so much attention from her.

'Shouldn't we move him?' I asked. 'He'd be better off at the other hospital.'

'Maybe. Maybe. But we can't move him now. His condition is too serious.'

'You do realize,' I said, 'that they might come back for him.'

It was the first time I'd realized it myself.

'Who?' she said.

'His . . . people,' I said. 'The people he was with.'

She looked at me in startled amazement. She didn't know what people I meant or why they would want to take him. But she didn't ask me more; in a moment she was back at her fussing. But the thought stayed with me for the rest of the day. Why would they leave him here if he knew all their secrets?

This had obviously occurred to Colonel Moller too, because the next morning Tehogo was chained to the bed and one of the soldiers was on guard in the corner.

I was on duty that day. When Dr Ngema came to do ward rounds she was astounded at the new security arrangements which had taken place without her. She rattled the silver handcuffs on Tehogo's wrist and glared at the soldier.

'Who are you? What are you doing here?'

He was a young white man, just out of adolescence, with a feathery moustache and a sardonic smile. Amused at her shock.

'I am on guard,' he said.

'Guard? Guarding who?'

Maybe he thought; this was too obvious to answer.

'He's under intensive care,' Dr Ngema said severely. 'Only medical staff are allowed in here.'

'You must talk to my colonel.'

'You can't chain him like this. This isn't a police state any more. Why are you doing this?'

'Danger.'

'Danger?' And she looked around the room, as if it might have taken on form: danger, a measurable quantity, hiding under the bed. 'I will complain. You can't do this. I will protest.'

But if she did complain or protest, nothing happened; the silver bracelet and the soldier stayed in place. Though he—the guard—moved at some point into the office with me. It was more companionable for him there, maybe, and he had the coffee and dartboard to distract him. And the truth was that I was glad to have him there. Not for company: it was the gun that consoled me. Since my talk with Dr Ngema the day before, I felt afraid.

But the soldier looked bored. He didn't seem to believe in the danger he'd mentioned. He didn't come with me when I went up and down the passage to the ward. Perhaps he thought this anxiety and attention were the normal state of things, whereas, in reality, no medical problem had ever preoccupied me so entirely.

At first Tehogo was completely still, like a corpse laid out for viewing. His position only changed when he was moved. I had to turn him every couple of hours because of bedsores. When I slid my hands under him to do this, my face came down close to his, so that I could smell his sour breath, coming up from the depths of an empty stomach. He was hot and limp and sweaty in my hands.

I had to do everything for him. Food and air were going into him through plastic tubes. I had to monitor the ventilator and keep an eye on the IV drip. Inject him with morphine every couple of hours. A urinary catheter had been inserted and the bag had to be emptied a couple of times. Later in the day he soiled himself and I had to change the sheets and wash him. All of these necessary labours were chores that Tehogo himself used to carry out. It was new to me. I had never touched Tehogo in my life before, and now I found myself caught in this essential intimacy. If this was an allegory I would be learning humility; but it was only real life, unsettling and tacky and strange, and the emotions it stirred in me were not entirely humble.

But as the day went on his condition improved. By noon his heartbeat and blood pressure were almost normal. And later I came in to turn him and found that he had moved by himself. A slight shift, a change in the placement of hands and feet, but an unmistakable sign of life rising up to the surface.

And the movement continued. A little twitch here, a flicker there—until by evening he was starting to twist and gesture in his sleep.

To keep him from tearing out the tubes, I tied him to the bed with pieces of soft cloth. But these restraining bonds—on his legs and free arm—mimicked and mocked the real chain on his wrist. He was a patient and a captive at the same time; just as I was a doctor and the cause of his condition.

Guilt, guilt; and I paced up and down the passage, unable to sit for long. The other doctors also came by from time to time to check on him. The Santanders and Dr Ngema—also worried and afraid. But their anxiety came from not understanding, while I understood too well.

The only one who didn't come by was Laurence. I expected him the whole day, if only because duty was a virtuous reflex with him. But he only arrived in the evening, when it was time for his shift. He'd been in the room, he said, trying to plan for the clinic.

I'd forgotten until this moment that the clinic was happening. But surely, under the circumstances, it would be cancelled.

'No, no,' Laurence said intensely. 'I spoke to Dr Ngema today. She said we must go ahead.'

'But what about Tehogo?'

'Well, it's serious, of course . . . but life goes on, Frank. I don't need to tell you that.'

And I saw that—for the first time—there was a patient in the hospital Laurence didn't care about. He was perturbed and upset, but he wished Tehogo away: this was a setback to his own, more glorious project.

What had we come to at last? The familiar world was turned on its head. The nurse had become a patient. The dedicated and caring young doctor had eyes only for himself, while I, the bitter unbeliever, would have prayed if I thought it would help.

There might be a lesson in all this, if I could only find it.

Meanwhile I hovered nervously in the office, though my duty was over and weariness had set in.

'Why don't you get some sleep?' Laurence said eventually. 'You look worn out.'

'I'll go in a moment. I'm just waiting.'

'Waiting for what?'

'I don't know.'

He studied me, appraising me. 'I thought you didn't like Tehogo,' he said.

'I don't. But I don't want him to die.'

'Remember what you told me once. Symbols have got nothing to do with medicine.'

'What do you mean? Tehogo's not a symbol for me.'
'Are you sure about that?'

In the morning Tehogo was awake. His gaze rested on me, cool and liquid, unblinking. I could see myself reflected there, a double image, before his eyes slid away on to the floor.

Claudia Santander was on duty that day, but I told her that I would fill in for her. She was confused. 'No, no,' she kept saying. 'Clinic is tomorrow. I no want work tomorrow.'

'You don't have to. I'm not swapping duties with you. I just want to work today, no exchange, no strings attached.'

She didn't understand, but eventually she left me to it. So through that next day too I waited on Tehogo. Dr Ngema came by and took out the IV drip and disconnected him from the ventilator. These were signs of his rapid recovery. But the bullet was still in him and would have to be removed.

'We'll wait a day or two before we operate,' Dr Ngema said. 'Let him stabilize first. What do you think, Frank?'

'I think he should be moved to the other hospital.'

'But I'm sure we can take care of it here . . . He's much better now.'

She wanted my agreement, but I wanted him gone. I wanted him far from here, where they couldn't get him. 'I feel very strongly about it,' I said. 'Let me move him.'

'Well . . . All right.' She blinked uncertainly. 'But he's too weak at the moment.'

'Tomorrow then. I'll do it first thing.'

'It's the clinic tomorrow.'

I stared at her. 'But surely you're not going ahead with that? Surely it should be cancelled? Under the circumstances.'

'Oh, no. No, that isn't possible, Frank.' She looked troubled. 'It's too important for us, the minister is expecting it . . . Not at this late stage.'

'Well, I'll skip it,' I said angrily. 'I'll take him through.'

I wasn't asking; she could hear the vehemence in my voice. She was too bewildered to resist.

Tehogo listened to all this without a word. He was still too weak and sore to speak, but when Dr Ngema talked to him he nodded or shook his head. Yes, he was comfortable. Yes, he had a headache. No, he didn't need the bedpan.

'When he's a bit stronger, later, try to get him to talk,' Dr Ngema said. This was by way of a whispered aside in the office. 'Try to find out what happened to him.'

She said this with anxiety, but I could see she didn't want to question him herself. She was happy to leave this delicate task to me. But Tehogo wouldn't speak to me. Even through the weakness and the morphine, some memory of his rancour still persisted: when I talked to him his eyes made that same show of looking, then sliding away.

It didn't stop me. He was still my captive patient, chained to his bed. The cloths had been untied from his feet and one hand, but the handcuff was there, rattling whenever he moved. He saw it, and he saw the soldier in the corner.

There was a new man on duty today, a nervous-looking type who sat stolidly, rifle between his knees, watching. This one took his job seriously; he wasn't tempted by the office, with its coffee and darts. He watched me come in and out, in and out, on my various little missions.

Tehogo could eat now, only liquid food because the tubes had left his throat raw. So twice that day I carried soup in to him on a tray and fed it to him carefully, spoon by spoon. His mouth opened and accepted, but his eyes avoided me. He underwent all my other attentions with the same burning passivity. He was meek, but I could feel his real feelings, buried and secret, coming off him like a heat.

I had to help him to urinate too. Sitting side by side like old friends, my one arm draped across his shoulders to support him.

He closed his eyes to cover the humiliation, and he did that again later when I washed him. I cleaned his body section by section, as if both of us were machines—though we had never been less mechanical.

I didn't talk to him. Not even the questions Dr Ngema wanted me to ask, though I wanted the answers too. Only once did a few words escape me; I leaned close to him and whispered into his ear.

'I told you you're not my enemy, Tehogo,' I said. 'Would I treat my enemy like this?'

The soldier looked up sharply: what subversive information was being exchanged so softly? But Tehogo's face stayed sealed. He wasn't going to give me anything.

I think of that evening as the last one, the final night; though at the time it felt ordinary. There was no weight of destiny on anything, so that it is hard now to remember any particular detail. It was like so many other nights—like all the other nights I'd spent at the hospital, whittling my life away. I was very tired, I do remember that, as if I'd used up my energy out of all proportion to the work. So that when Laurence arrived for his duty, I didn't feel like hanging around any more. There was nothing to be anxious about, after all. In the morning I would be taking Tehogo away.

'Are you all set for tomorrow, Frank?' Laurence said cheerfully.

'For what? Oh, Laurence, I can't make the clinic. I have to move Tehogo.'

'But why tomorrow? Can't he wait another day?'

'No. I'm sorry. It's not possible.'

'Yes, of course. Of course. No problem. I didn't really think you'd come anyway.'

Was all this actually said, did we even have this conversation? I don't know; I may have added to the memory afterwards. It seems wrong—after all the important words—that the final words should be lost in banality.

So I remember, or I imagine, that the last time I saw Laurence his face had a trace of petulance in it. He pretended it didn't matter, but he was hurt all over again. I was letting him down one more time, just as he'd half-expected me to. I called out to say goodbye, but he occupied himself by rummaging about in the supply cupboard. My own voice, calling out his name, set up little shivery echoes in the empty passage.

And in the morning he was gone. So was the soldier, so was Tehogo. And to get around the little problem of the handcuffs, they had taken the bed too.

18

I had set the alarm to wake up early. As I crossed the open ground between the buildings, it was just past dawn. In the pale light I could see people at the main wing, coming and going.

Dr Ngema met me at the door. Her face was wooden; it took her a while to get her words out.

'They've gone,' she said. 'Gone.'

'Who? What do you mean?'

But I knew already, though I had to go down the passage to the deserted ward to understand. And even then I stared at the bare patch on the floor, slightly cleaner than the area around it, as if it contained a message that I might decipher in time.

And in a few minutes I became one of those aimless people who were coming and going, coming and going. There was no frenzy or focus to the movement. Everybody was in shock. It seemed astonishing that three human beings and a hospital bed could have vanished in the night. So silently, so completely without trace. As if a huge hand had reached down to sweep them all away.

How did it happen? How many of them were there, what weapons did they have? Did they drive in through the main gate, like visitors, or did they slip in over the wall like assassins? I didn't know; I could never know the answers to these questions, because it happened in another country, while I slept.

And Laurence—why had they taken him, what did he do to make his disappearance necessary? I could almost guess at this, although I hadn't seen it: he would have stood in their way, he would have inserted himself between Tehogo and the enemy. *I'm sorry, you can't take him, he is my patient. I have a duty to protect him.* Duty, honour, obligation—Laurence lived for words like these, and in the end he died for them too.

It could just as easily have been one of the other doctors doing their shift of duty that night; it could even have been me. And then it might have turned out differently. I didn't live for words like duty. Not many people do. It turned out, for example, that the soldier hadn't been taken. He'd run for his life when he saw them coming. Hours later he would return from the bush, trailing his shame and his rifle. The bed would also be recovered, disassembled and broken into pieces in the grass; only one end of it, the part where Tehogo had been chained, never came back.

But all of this was later, in the logical stage of explanation and reason. There was no logic or reason that morning. There was only the long lonely passage, and that blank space in the ward, like a pulled tooth.

Dr Ngema was one of the aimless bodies. She turned to me later with obvious desperation.

'It's unbelievable. I can't believe it. Frank, what shall we do?'

'I don't know,' I said dully. 'Report it.'

'I have. I spoke to that man, that army man. He said he'd do everything in his power . . .'

'Then there's nothing more you can do.'

'He said I should write everything up in a report. All the facts. I'll have to do that later. After the clinic.'

'You're still going to the clinic?'

'What can we do?' she cried. 'It's all arranged!'

And soon afterwards they disappeared—the three of them that were left, the Santanders and Dr Ngema. They were going to do their duty at the gathering where electricity was being connected for the first time. I think they thought I would be following them in my own car, but I didn't follow. I wandered up and down the passage, and then up and down the upstairs passage too, and then outside, in the grass.

It felt to me that he was still out there somewhere, close by, alive. Laurence—with his ideals and his sense of duty. Of course maybe he wasn't; he may already have been lying in a ditch or a shallow grave, with his throat cut or a bullet in his head—whatever happened to him in the end. I have tried, since then, to imagine it—his final moments, the climax of his story—but on that day the pictures wouldn't come. Being murdered and thrown away like a piece of rubbish: that was something that happened to other people, people one didn't know, not to Laurence. No, he was out there, not too far away, keeping his outrage and hope alive. Waiting for somebody to help him—because that was what people did: they helped each other.

And so it was coming to me at last: my moment, if not of truth, then at least of action. Too late, all the connections missed. But my life was finally yielding up an instant of real courage. I didn't know it yet; I could only sense a gathering power, which felt as yet somewhere outside of me, and even when I got into my car and drove out of the gate I had no clear idea of where I was going.

This time I took the turning and lurched and bumped down the rutted dirt road. I knew by then, of course; in the way that you might deduce a man's intentions by watching what he was doing. The occasion was rising in me and I could already see my arrival: driving at speed through the front gate, wheels churning up a cloud of dust and valour and high drama around me. But down at the bottom of the little dip my car hit a rock and stalled and it wouldn't start again. My momentum was dissipating and before it could leave me completely I got out and staggered at a half-run up the slope. I saw how I would go in amongst all the amazed faces to the one face that mattered and fall on my knees in front of him.

I am here, I would say, *to offer myself in exchange. Not for Tehogo—he's one of you, take him. For the other one. He is nothing to you, I know that, but to me he has become everything. Everything, at least, that I am not. Character is fate, it is my fate to have done nothing with my life, except to watch and judge and find everything wanting, so allow me in my final moment to transform myself. I beg you, take me in his place, give me a death that will make sense of my life, do what you want with me, but let him go.*

I would have. I would have said it all. In that moment I wasn't afraid to die.

But of course they weren't there; I don't know why I thought they would be. They must have left the camp for good when Tehogo was shot, and there was no reason ever to come back. It was only in my mind that they were fixed in one place, like a target at which I had aimed my life like an arrow. But I had missed again. I couldn't even summon up a proper tragedy from all the promising raw material of my life.

So there was nothing to face up to in the end, except the ridiculous figure that was myself. Heavy, long past his prime, gasping for breath. Standing doubled-over in the centre of this deserted theatre, watched only by rotten canvas and rusted barbed wire.

And him. After a few minutes he appeared, looking calm and a bit bored, strolling over from the far side of the camp, where I only now saw the top of his jeep sticking up.

He was wearing his uniform again. But his bearing today was casual, more civilian than military. He had his hands in his pockets and he was whistling through his teeth.

'Good morning, Doctor,' he said.

He didn't seem surprised to see me there. Only a little amused at how sweaty I was.

'You need some basic training,' he said. 'That'll get you into shape.'

'I came . . .' I said. 'I came . . . to look . . .'

'Me too. Your boss, that doctor lady, told me what happened. So I thought it was time to check out your story. See if there was anything here. But . . .'

He gestured at the decay around us, the brown weeds pushing through the ground.

'It's not true,' I said. 'You've been here before. Why do you go on denying it?'

He smiled thinly; he was in a good mood today. 'But there's nobody here. Except us. And it's a *kak* place.'

'What will happen now?'

'Nothing. They've gone. I don't think we'll be seeing them again.'

'I meant . . . what will happen to him? To my friend.'

'I was talking about your friend,' he said.

And then there was nothing more to say. It had all run out here, in the unlikeliest of places, on an ordinary day.

'How did you get here?' he said. 'Can I give you a lift?'

'My car's down there. It's stuck.'

'I'll come and give you a hand. Let me just get my jeep.'

He started to turn away, whistling again, but I said, 'Commandant.'

I don't know where it came from, this pointless need to tell the truth.

'You mean Colonel,' he said.

'I know you from before. Do you remember?'

It was extraordinary how his face changed. He was instantly alert. Something in him contracted to that hard core, tiny and closed and impregnable. He was watching me as if from a long way off.

'Where was that?'

'Up on the border.' I named the camp and the year. I saw his mind fix on that time in his head, then on my face, trying to fit the two together.

'I was working as a medic,' I said. 'You used to call on the captain sometimes to help you. But one night the captain wasn't there and you called me instead.'

'You helped me?'

'Yes.'

He stared at me for a moment longer and then he lost interest. I could see it happen. There was no danger to him; I was just a piece of flotsam after all.

'Sorry,' he said. 'I don't remember.'

'But we spoke to each other.'

'Maybe so. I spoke to a lot of people up there. I'm sorry.'

His tone was brisk and detached. He wasn't interested any more. I had made my little confession, but he couldn't give me absolution. Acting on an impulse that I didn't understand, I took two steps towards him and held out my hand. He shook it. The gesture was nothing, an empty formality; the real transaction had happened a long time ago.

19

Laurence will never come back. I know that now. But for the first few days, even though I was alone again in my room, it didn't feel that way. Laurence's clothes were still strewn around, hanging over the back of the chair and on the rail in the bathroom; his half-smoked cigarette lay among ash on the windowsill; all the signs indicated that he was just out for a while, on duty or somewhere, and he would be back in a moment.

But after a week or so, on an impulse one day, I tidied away all his things. I gathered together the little shrine he'd built on the windowsill, with the photographs and stones. I folded his clothes into a pile and put all of it into his suitcase—the one he'd been carrying when he arrived—and stored it under the bed. I wiped and cleaned away all the scuffs and marks, the shaving foam on the mirror, the cigarette stubs. I took his tooth-brush out of the holder in the bathroom and, after reflection, I threw it away.

Things felt a bit better then. I was nearly alone again. And when one day, a week or two later, I had the sudden inspiration to move the furniture around, back to the way it was before he came, it was almost as if he'd never been there.

Though he had. I knew that too. And there was the other empty bed to accuse me.

Amongst the few papers he had, I found a letter from Zanele, on the back of which was a return address in Lesotho. I wasn't sure if I should write, but then I did. Nobody else might've told her. This was a difficult job. I thought it would be simple—just a blunt statement of fact—but the facts themselves resisted me. I wrote down that he was dead, and then I sat staring at the word. *Dead.* It seemed to have a meaning that didn't apply in this case. There was no body, no weapon, no clear set of events. In the end I wrote only that he had disappeared, under bizarre and extreme circumstances, and that I would explain if she contacted me.

She didn't contact me. Maybe she never got the letter—she might have been back in America by then—or she may not have wanted to know more. I didn't know what else I could do to follow up, and the truth is that I was relieved not to know.

I looked through his letters for a home address, but there wasn't one. The envelopes that had come from his sister—who was really his mother—didn't have a return address on them. I asked Dr Ngema if she had anything on file, and she told me that she had already attended to it. Again, I was relieved not to be involved.

Then his mother arrived one day. This was one or two months after he'd gone. She was a tall, gaunt woman in a black trouser-suit, chain-smoking cigarettes in a long holder. I couldn't put her together with Laurence at all. There was something of the broad face that I remembered, but the manner and the looseness of her gestures were strange. She spent a good few hours stalking around the hospital grounds, peering into weedy corners, looking over the wall. She gave the impression of someone searching with calm determination in all the wrong places for something she had lost.

Eventually she came to sit in the room with me. Dr Ngema, who wanted nothing to do with any difficult emotions, asked me if I would see to her. 'This is Laurence's sister,' she said hurriedly. 'She wants to chat to you for a while.' I didn't mind; I was even curious, in a painful way. But when we were facing each other, she on his bed, I on mine, the way that he and I used to talk, there was suddenly nothing to say. Instead of an awkward scene, we seemed to have been brought together by a vacuum.

I took out his suitcase and the little heap of photographs and gave them to her. She picked through them listlessly.

'I've got the keys for his car too,' I said. 'You'll want to take that, I'm sure.'

'Oh, no, no. Not now. I'm here in my own car.'

'It's just standing out there. I start it up from time to time.'

'That's good of you. I'll come and get it soon.' She looked around, her dark eyes darker in their pale saucers of bone. 'So this is where . . .' she said, 'where . . .'

'Yes?'

'This was his room.'

'He stayed here with me. Yes.'

She looked directly at me. She was a frail woman, who seemed almost to have been glued together, and only her smoke-roughened voice gave an indication of some of the harshness of her life. That, and something in her eyes.

'You were his friend,' she said.

'Sorry?'

'He told me. He wrote about you often in his letters.'

'Did he? I'm touched by that. But I don't know how good I was as a friend.'

'Oh, you were. Don't run yourself down. I could tell by the way he spoke about you . . . He said you took care of him.'

'Really,' I said. 'Yes, I suppose I was his friend.'

'Thank you for being good to my... to my little brother.'

The whole act was absurd, and doubly absurd now. I couldn't help myself. I said, 'I know you're his mother. There's no point in concealing it.'

She didn't flinch—just nodded calmly, puffing on her cigarette. 'He told you, I suppose.'

'Well, I . . . yes.'

'That shows how much he trusted you. He would never have told you otherwise.'

I didn't know how to answer that. I wished she would go, but she seemed to have taken root here in the room. A silence spread while she puffed and puffed, and then she said suddenly, 'I don't understand how this happened.'

I felt a quickening in myself, as if all the pretence was finally dropping.

'It's a very complicated set of events.'

'So you do understand.'

'No, I . . . Not really, no.'

'But he's disappeared.'

'Yes.'

'He's not dead. He's disappeared. That's not the same thing.'

'I'm not sure that I follow you.'

She was still calm and imperturbable; I watched as she dumped the old cigarette out of the window and fitted a new one into the holder. 'What I mean is,' she said, 'he may come back.'

Her voice was level, and I thought she was making a statement. But her eyes stayed fixed on me and I realized that it was a question.

I thought about it for a moment, then I said, 'No. I don't think so.'

And she started to cry. It was astonishing: that long, passion-less frame, yielding up so much jagged emotion. She dropped her face into her hands and sobbed. I went to sit next to her and put an arm around her. It tore something in my heart and I was sorry that we'd arrived, after all, at this moment of genuine feeling.

Laurence was gone. He'd disappeared. And in a certain way she was right: that is not the same thing as dying.

Other people went away later. They disappeared, but not like Laurence: they went off into the labyrinths of their own lives. After a few months the soldiers were posted somewhere else and Colonel Moller went with them. One night they were there around the pool table, drinking and swaggering, and the next night it had all gone quiet.

Then Claudia Santander went back to Cuba. What had happened with Laurence was somehow the last straw for their marriage. There was no more fighting through the wall, but the silence instead was heavy and colourless. It was obvious that they weren't speaking to each other any more and then, at one of the Monday meetings, it was announced that she was leaving next week. So the rupture came at last. When she was gone it was just the two of us in the passage, Jorge and me, and the hours of duty became very long.

Dr Ngema left at almost the same time, back to the city and the post in the Department she'd been wanting. This was supposed to be a good departure, for her and for me. And of course it was. But there was a final conversation with Dr Ngema that I can't forget, which seemed to rise up out of nowhere.

It was in her office, on one of the last afternoons before she left. She was showing me what the job involved, the reporting and auditing and filing. At one point she was telling me how to go about applying for funding to get extra staff to replace the people we'd lost. This was a crisis for the hospital, obviously, that had to be dealt with urgently. But it reminded us both of more personal feelings and in the middle of some long, dry explanation she went abruptly quiet. Then she sighed and said, 'Poor Tehogo.'

'What?'

'What happened to him was terrible. It was a terrible thing.'

I could have left it; I could have let it go. But something turned in me. As she went back to her papers I said: 'And Laurence?'

She blinked, looking startled. 'Yes. And Laurence too.'

'Tehogo is still alive,' I said. 'I don't think Laurence is alive.'

She put the papers down slowly and looked at me. The air between us had thickened.

'I don't know what you mean,' she said.

'I mean Tehogo is one of them. They came to get him so he wouldn't talk. But they won't harm him.'

'"They,"' she said. 'Who are "they"?'

'His people.'

'Tehogo didn't have any people. He was alone. If you want to know, I think the soldiers took him. He saw something they didn't want him to see.'

I clucked my tongue in disbelief. 'He wasn't a victim,' I said. 'Why must you believe he was?'

Now she smiled, but without a trace of amusement.

'You never liked Tehogo,' she said slowly. 'You had it in for him from a long time ago.'

'That isn't true.'

'I'm sorry, Frank, but I think it is. You wanted him out. You wanted him gone. You couldn't deal with him. Well, now he's gone.'

'He hasn't. He's out there somewhere.'

'You're very sure of everything.'

'I know who Tehogo was. He was a thief, I saw what he did. I was disappointed in you, that you protected him.'

All of this was spoken very coldly and politely between us, as though we were discussing some abstract point. There had been a lot of times lately when Dr Ngema and I had talked sharply to each other. But this wasn't like those times.

'That young man,' she said, 'that young man had a very hard life. A very difficult life. Much more difficult than yours. None of your chances, none of your advantages. Doesn't that count with you?'

'Not in this case. No.'

'No. I can see it doesn't.' She was looking at me, but also past me, at something beyond me. 'I can see you have no idea of what it means to be a black person in this country. Only your own life is real to you.'

'That's true of everybody. You can only live one life.'

'Black people live many lives.'

'What rubbish.'

'Yes. To you it is rubbish. To me it is real. But there is no point in talking like this.'

She bent over the papers again and the conversation slipped out of sight, into a pocket somewhere, like a hard little knife. But it had cut us both. We never mentioned it again and in our last few meetings we were carefully nice to each other.

*   *   *

Maria had disappeared too, but then she came back. I had given up long before of ever seeing her again. Until one day a young black man, vaguely familiar, turned up at the office. He could take me to what I wanted, he said.

It took me a while to understand what he was talking about. Then I remembered where I'd seen him before: in the village behind Maria's shack, on the day that I'd gone there to look for her. He was the one who translated my message for me, when I offered money in exchange for any help they could give me.

I couldn't go with him then. I was on duty. And it would be a good few days before I was free to go. Then I went to get him and we drove together in my car, with him sitting next to me, pointing out the way with shy confidence, beaming to himself. It was a long trip on back roads—on the network of dirt tracks that led off from the main route. The countryside here was wild and tangled, giving way occasionally to one of those nameless villages that were just a spray of dots on Laurence's map.

And she was in one of those dots, somewhere close to the line of blue hills on the horizon. The car struggled up the last stretch, up a terrible track that seemed to have been cut out of the bush with a blunt blade just the day before. Up at the top of the hill was the straggle of huts and fields. Nothing to differentiate it from any of the others we'd passed, but the beaming young man said, 'Here.'

'Here?'

He showed me where to go. One of the last huts at the edge of the village, a wall of trees behind. And outside, the white car.

I had always seen it in passing, from a distance. But when I walked past it now I could see that this car had nothing to do with the Brigadier. It was an old Datsun, rusted right through all over the bonnet and roof. One door was hanging loosely and there was a crack across the windscreen. It was a poor man's car.

So the puzzle, the picture that lay just out of my reach, was not complete after all. Or the pieces did not all fit together in the way I thought they did.

And the same, maybe, could be said about Maria. I assumed that she knew I was coming—that the young man, my guide, would have spoken to her, would have told her I was looking for her. But the moment I saw her I knew that I had dropped out of the sky.

This was behind the little hut, in a bare patch next to the trees. When I knocked at the front door a man's voice called out from the back and we went around. She was sitting down, but she jumped up to her feet, a hand clapped to her mouth. Staring at me.

He was there too. This was the first time I saw him. The man. About my age, squat, with a round face and a checked cap slanted on his head. He didn't seem the type to display much feeling, but I could sense his astonishment, like a vibration through the ground.

So we were all standing there, looking at each other. Three of us transfixed by a kind of dismay, and the other one still incongruously beaming.

I said, 'Maria.'

But it wasn't even her name, not her real name. She turned sharply away from me, to her husband, and started speaking to him. Rapidly, in a high voice. I didn't understand any of it. Then she broke off, turned and ran into the house without a backward glance.

I don't know what I expected: that we would sit around in a happy reunion, talking about old times. That somehow the man wouldn't be there, as he had conveniently been absent while our affair went on. Or that we would be miraculously restored to the square of sand in the shack, with darkness outside.

But it wasn't going to be like that. This was a story without a resolution—maybe even without a theme. I was only here to learn again how much I didn't know and would never understand.

The man was very angry. He came up and talked at me in a low, steady, pushy voice. His fists were bunched up at his sides but I didn't think he would use them. Not yet. He was too surprised, too unsure of himself still.

'I don't know what he's telling me,' I said.

'He say,' the young man translated, 'what do you want here?'

'I wanted to speak to Maria.'

'He say, what do you want with his wife?'

'Tell him nothing. Nothing bad. I am her friend, from before, from the shop. I wanted to find out if she is okay.'

'He say, she is okay. He say you better go now.'

'I am not here to make trouble. Tell him that.'

But my arrival here had made trouble. It had brewed up around me, like the fine dust being lifted by the wind. It was better to leave, without knowing what would happen behind me, and we did, a minute or two later. All the long way home again, after a visit of two or three minutes.

'But she is alive,' I said aloud to myself. This was maybe half an hour later, as we sped along some arbitrary stretch of road. 'At least I know that.'

'Yes,' my companion agreed happily. 'She is alive.'

And that was something. All the rest of it I couldn't know. She had sat at the core of my life, like a cryptic symbol, but to her I was just a background detail, bringing mystery and disturbance. I would never see her again, but she was alive.

When we got back and I dropped the young man off, he hovered expectantly by the car. I was so preoccupied that it took me a minute to understand. Then I took out my wallet.

I had set out with the idea of giving some money to Maria, and this sheaf of notes was folded up, close to hand. After a hesitation I took the little wad out and gave all of it to him. It was a large sum, more than I had ever given away before. I don't know what I had in mind: to buy her back, or to make my final disappearance worthwhile.

He looked astounded for a second, then he quickly put it away. His smile was radiant.

Shortly before the cancer finally took him, my father told me he wanted to come up and visit me. I think it was his way of showing approval. When I told him I'd become head of the hospital at last, he said, 'Oh, thank God.' He was imagining a different scenario to this. I didn't enlighten him and it was a relief, in the end, that he was too weak to make the trip. He went thinking that I'd finally turned the corner, that I'd arrived somewhere. And on paper I suppose I have.

Things are different now, in lots of obvious ways. For one thing, I work in Dr Ngema's office. Instead of the dart board and the hours of boredom there is a desk and paperwork in front of me. I don't feel much like a doctor any more; I have become an administrator.

The hospital is in trouble and it is my job now to save it. Letters and phone calls go back and forth. The Department wants to close us down and I spend a lot of time explaining why that is a bad idea. We are doing vital work in poor rural communities, I tell them. Ironically, I have had to use the example of the two clinics that Laurence ran to bolster my own argument.

We are not running any field clinics now. We are not doing very much of anything, in fact. There are only two doctors left, the same number as the kitchen staff—one cook for each of us. And I don't know how much longer Jorge will stay.

So we have had to scale down on all fronts. We have become, in effect, a day clinic, open for a couple of hours every morning. Mostly we dispense medicine and advice. Any serious cases, or even not-so-serious ones that would involve an overnight stay, are referred elsewhere.

So the situation is dire and the prospects not good. But still— although I can't logically explain it—I am content. Maybe this is only the false peace of resignation. But I feel, somehow, that I have come into my own.

This might be just because, after seven years of waiting, I have shifted about twenty metres away, into Dr Ngema's room. A small event, but it means a lot to me. A new room, bare and clean and empty: a good place to start again. I spread my things around and bought a few cloths and pictures to hang up. Any-thing to stamp myself on to the blankness. And now my life has taken root again. I know I won't be stuck here for ever; other places, other people, will follow on.

A whole new sense of the future, because of one tiny change. Which makes me wonder if all of this might have happened differently if I'd never had to share my room.

THIS IS NO LONGER THE PROPERTY
OF THE SEATTLE PUBLIC LIBRARY

9 780802 141699